Stories by Contemporary Writers from Shanghai

HIS
ONE AND ONLY

Copyright © 2010 Shanghai Press and Publishing Development
Company

This book is edited and designed by the Editorial Committee of
Cultural China series

Managing Directors: Wang Youbu, Xu Naiqing
Editorial Director: Wu Ying
Series Editor: Wang Jiren
Editors: Daniel Clutton, Ye Jiasheng

Text by Wang Xiaoyu
Translation by Yang Shuhui, Yang Yunqin

Interior and Cover Design: Wang Wei
Cover Image: Getty Images

ISBN: 978-1-60220-214-6

Address any comments about *His One and Only* to:

Better Link Press
99 Park Ave
New York, NY 10016
USA
or
Shanghai Press and Publishing Development Company
F 7 Donghu Road, Shanghai, China (200031)
Email: comments_betterlinkpress@hotmail.com

Printed in China by Shanghai Donnelley Printing Co. Ltd.

1 2 3 4 5 6 7 8 9 10

HIS
ONE AND ONLY

By Wang Xiaoyu

Better Link Press

Preface

English readers will be presented with a set of 12 pocket books. These books contain outstanding novellas written by 12 writers from Shanghai over the past 30 years. Most of the writers were born in Shanghai from the late 1940's to the late 1950's. They started their literary careers during or after the 1980's. For various reasons, most of them lived and worked in the lowest social strata in other cities or in rural areas for much of their adult lives. As a result they saw much of the world and learned lessons from real life before finally returning to Shanghai. They embarked on their literary careers for various reasons, but most of them were simply passionate about writing. The writers are involved in a variety of occupations, including university professors, literary editors, leaders of literary institutions and professional writers. The diversity of topics covered in these novellas will lead readers to discover the different experiences and motivations of the authors. Readers will encounter a fascinating range of esthetic convictions as they analyze the authors' distinctive artistic skills and writing styles. Generally speaking, a realistic writing style dominates most of their literary works. The literary works they have elaborately created are a true reflection of drastic social changes, as well as differing perspectives towards urban life in Shanghai. Some works created by avant-garde writers have been selected in order to present a variety of styles. No matter what writing styles they adopt though, these writers have enjoyed a definite place, and exerted a positive influence, in Chinese literary circles over the past three decades.

Known as the "Paris of the Orient" around the world, Shanghai was already an international metropolis in the 1920's and 1930's. During that period, Shanghai was China's economic, cultural and literary center. A high number of famous Chinese writers lived, created and published their literary works in Shanghai, including, Lu Xun, Guo Moruo, Mao Dun and Ba Jin. Today, Shanghai has become a globalized metropolis. Writers who have pursued a literary career in the past 30 years are now faced with new challenges and opportunities. I am confident that some of them will produce other fine and influential literary works in the future. I want to make it clear that this set of pocket books does not include all representative Shanghai writers. When the time is ripe, we will introduce more representative writers to readers in the English-speaking world.

Wang Jiren
Series Editor

Contents

Part III

Conclusion

Prelude

The promotion was officially announced. I was a professor.

Although only one month short of fifty, I was nevertheless fortunate enough to have made the list of "Outstanding young and middle-aged people due for promotion on an exceptional basis on account of their extraordinary contributions." My department offered me a new three-bedroom apartment with complete bathroom facilities and a kitchen with a gas range. It was at the top end of on-campus apartments owned by the college.

So I would soon be moving. Books and the files were to be tied up in stacks, and piles of index cards stuffed into large brown envelopes.

All of a sudden, my hand slipped and more than a thousand cards scattered all over the floor. My wife Xiangzhu picked up the first one that lay in front of her and saw on it the following entry: "The laws of the Qing dynasty allowed the emperor to have one empress, one royal consort, two high consorts, four consorts, six secondary consorts, and a number of titled ladies-in-waiting."

With a chuckle, Xiangzhu said, "What's the use of this information? Don't we all know that emperors had their harems?"

She picked up another card. "Emperor Kangxi (1662–1722) was on the throne for sixty years and died at age sixty-nine. He had fifty-five titled consorts and thirty-five sons in total. His tomb, the Jing Mausoleum, was built at what is now known as the Eastern Mausoleums of the Qing emperors. Five of his consorts were later buried with him, two were placed in the Two Consorts' Tomb and the other forty-eight were put in the Consorts' Tomb in the Jing Mausoleum."

"My goodness!" exclaimed Xiangzhu. "He

had enough wives to make up a whole class!"

Xiangzhu was teaching a graduating class in a "key" elementary school. The fifty-six children of her class filled the classroom to overflowing.

"Emperor Qianlong of the Qing dynasty had forty-one consorts."

"Emperor Chengzu (1360–1424) of the Ming dynasty, Zhu Di, fourth son of Emperor Taizu, Zhu Yuanzhang, took the throne after defeating Emperor Jianwen and ruled for twenty-two years. Upon his death, more than thirty of his consorts were killed and buried with him. Here's how the whole process went: They were first treated to a banquet and then driven into a room. Each was ordered to stand on a wooden bed and put her neck through a noose. It was all over for them after the eunuchs moved the beds away. The house shook with wails of grief that were heart-rending to hear."

Xiangzhu picked up another two cards from the floor and began reading again, "Zhu An, known as Madam Zhu, married Lu Xun (1881–1936) at age nineteen. Of a gentle disposition, she excelled at managing the household. After Lu Xun relocated to Shanghai with Xu Guangping as his new wife, Madam Zhu lived with Lu Xun's mother, administering to her needs. She remained childless."

"Kang Youwei (1858–1927) had six wives in total, of whom the fourth one, Tsuruko, was Japanese and forty years younger than Kang. Kang Youwei's son Kang Tongjian, of the same age as his stepmother, soon committed incest and had a daughter with her. The daughter, Ayako, now lives in Japan."

Inquiringly Xiangzhu turned toward me and said, looking me in the eye, "Why are these index cards all devoted to the same subject, may I ask?"

"Ah yes, most of them belong to the same category. Actually, it had never occurred to me that …"

Xiangzhu gave me a meaningful smile that was devoid of humor and said, "Maybe your subconscious is up to some funny business."

"Well, I'm beginning to think along the same lines …"

She rose and said, slapping her behind, "Too bad!" As she turned away, she added, "Too bad you were born a hundred years too late! Nor were you reincarnated as an emperor's offspring ..."

Only then did I catch the bitterness in her tone. Oh women!

She would hardly be blamed. We had been married for twenty years, but I had still not let her in on every secret of our Xuan clan. There was a sense of shame hidden in my subconscious, a sense that led to my secretive ways of doing things and directed my attention to a specific kind of information. Before I knew it, I had put by hundreds of index cards that, like a focusing glass, zeroed in on the most sensitive spot in my subconscious. The deepest hidden secret was exactly what triggered off the greatest excitement. You see, the Xuan family may not have produced kings and princes or generals and ministers, nor was it part of a tribe living in remote regions, but there had nonetheless been more than one concubine in the family, and I, a newly-promoted full professor of history, am the son of my father's second concubine. I had been keeping this secret of secrets from Xiangzhu for twenty years. When she insinuated that I was having improper thoughts, Xiangzhu inadvertently hit a very raw nerve by awakening my "subconscious."

By evening, all our household articles had been moved into the new apartment. The only items remaining in the third-floor attic were the large bed and its straw mat that was still covered with my index cards. The bed was to be used that night. The cards were still there because I had been flipping through them for the last few hours. With an ever so slight look of disgust, Xiangzhu did not so much as touch them. I never paid much mind to her hypersensitivity, just as she always put up with my failings. Before turning off the lights, I gathered her in my arms and said that it was time I told her something about my family history. I added that what I was going to say had everything to do with the index cards.

"Really?" she exclaimed, her sleepiness all

gone. She was a regular viewer of late-night movies.

Part I

1

My Grandfather and My Eldest Brother

As you know, my ancestral home is in Anhui. My eldest brother is still there. Haven't you met him once? When my father was critically ill last year, my eldest sister sent him a telegram and he came. True, he doesn't bear the slightest resemblance to other members of the family, not even to Big Sister who was born to the same mother. He takes after my grandfather. All my other siblings and I inherited, from our father, our grandmother's aquiline nose. Among us, Big Brother is the only one whose nose, like Grandpa's, was anything but aquiline.

I have seen Grandpa once, after his death.

I went with my father to the funeral sometime in April or May in 1966. Grandpa's body lay in the middle of the main hall. He was properly attired, with a brand new Mao suit, a pair of blue khaki pants, and a cadre's cap, looking every bit like a production brigade cadre. In fact, he was a farmer through and through, without ever having held any official titles in his life, not even anything that would remotely resemble one, such as a "keeper" of something, a "poultry raiser," or a "chef" in a cafeteria. All his life he tilled the land and he grew only wheat and corn in what was called at that time an endeavor to "make grain the key in agricultural production." What he was wearing had been bought and put on him by my eldest brother after his death. Retro was not in fashion as it is now. Whereas the deceased now wear tailor-made silk clothes, silk hats, and silk shoes, and even hold silk handkerchiefs in their hands, in that era a Mao suit was the height of glory for the deceased and the best that the living could offer them.

My grandfather lay on a plank bed, looking

peaceful. His nose was anything but aquiline.

"Grandpa! Oh Grandpa! I'm the only one left in this place now! Oh!" My eldest brother, wearing mourning white, was kneeling in front of the shrine next to the bed and sobbing bitterly. He was the only one without an aquiline nose among members of my generation, and he was thin and small, just as Grandpa had been, whereas the rest of us are, one and all, broad-shouldered and of vigorous build. Even my little sister weighs more than 130 catties. His face washed with tears, Big Brother was chanting his wails of grief in the manner of the local village women. This was partly because, having been born and raised there, he was steeped in the local customs, and partly because he took after my grandfather in disposition and lacked the strength of character that my father had inherited from my grandmother and had, in turn, passed on to me and to my other siblings.

I went up to the shrine with my father to kowtow to Grandpa's spiritual tablet as well as the peanuts, wild water chestnuts, and the salted duck placed in front of it. The replacement of the usual three kinds of sacrificial meat (beef, mutton, and pork) by these three items took me by surprise, but after spending the next couple of days with my folks, sharing their meals, accommodation, and hardships, I came to realize that the villagers had nothing better to offer to the souls of the departed. An able-bodied laborer was paid seventeen cents per day, and the daily ration of grain was less than one catty per person. Their breakfast fare consisted of nothing more than salted chives, all mushy and brownish, to go with cooked flour paste. Lunch, the best meal of the day, consisted of a large bowl of noodles with a sprinkling of soy sauce plus two or three droplets of cooked oil. Supper was porridge, so watery that it could function as a mirror. Peanuts and wild water chestnuts were a luxury that frugal and hardworking parents offered as a treat to children only on New Year's Day. As for the saltier-than-salt ducks that had been air-dried until the meat was harder than wood and darker than charcoal, they were nothing less than delicacies hung from the rafter in the main hall of every household in a show of wealth, and were reluctantly served at the dinner table only upon the appearance of the most honored guests. The very fact that Grandpa's shrine was graced by these three kinds of offerings was proof enough of Big Brother's filial devotion.

While my father and I were paying homage to the shrine, Big Brother's lamentations grew all the more vehement.

"Grandpa!" he wailed. "I'm now all alone! I am the only luckless one!"

At the time, these plaintive cries sounded to my ears more like accusations, with my father as their object. Although I was only twenty-six or twenty-seven years old and had just graduated and been offered a job in the same college as a faculty member, I had already learned all there was to know about the history of the Xuan clan. With my unique perceptiveness and insight in these matters, I was able to detect the deep-down bitterness in my big brother's ritualistic lamentations. I stole a glance at my father in his kneeling position. He was in his fifties, in the prime of life. His cheeks were not yet sunken, as they are now. I remember how he kept his lips tightly pressed, and moved his jawbones, with his tearless eyes flashing fire and the corner of his mouth visible to me twitching slightly. Rather than grief-stricken over his father's death, he looked more like a man making an effort to control his temper as he listened to my eldest brother whose bitter tone was certainly not lost on him.

But in fact, who can hold anything against Big Brother? His resentment against my father is quite understandable. As he saw it, who else but my father was responsible for the unhappy state he was in? Of the ten of us siblings, nine were on the government payroll. He was the only one left behind in that impoverished village. While he was wresting a miserable livelihood from the soil for seventeen cents a day, my father was living the good life of a factory-owner in the land of abundance south of the lower reaches of the Yangtze River, taking in one wife after another, and ignoring him—the eldest son of the principal wife, ignoring his mother—who had married into the Xuan family the proper way, through the mediation of a matchmaker, and ignoring his grandfather—who had managed to sport a decent Mao suit only after his death. Would anyone not nurse a grudge against such a father? My big brother may be an honest, meek, and inarticulate person, qualities that he inherited from Grandpa, but he is no less of a person than everybody else, with feelings of happiness, anger, grief, and joy as well as the elevated IQ of the Xuan clan. How could he possibly be unaware of his father's decades-long frostiness to him, to his mother, and even to Grandpa who had never worn clothes without a darn until after his death? Big Brother would never forget that Father had almost never paid a visit home since he was born, at least since he began to understand something of the world. He would never forget that only his elder sister, born to the same mother, had sent him eight or ten yuan every month while Father had never given him a penny for decades. He would not forget that, in 1958, when the Great Leap

Forward was sweeping across the country, city and village alike, he had written to Father with a plea to find him a job as a factory worker in the city so that he could leave behind his life as a peasant, as so many of his young fellow villagers had done, but Father never even bothered to write him a reply. Standing out foremost in his memory was what had happened about two years after the onset of the Great Leap Forward: Somehow the village had run out of food. So Grandpa sent Father a message, asking him to mail some grain coupons to save a few lives. By the time Father sent, one month later, fifteen-catties-worth of national grain coupons that could be used to buy grain anywhere in the country, Big Brother's mother had already died of a diet of white clay, and his wife of less than three years, unable to tolerate the harsh life anymore, had eloped with another man. Grandpa survived on what little ration his deceased daughter-in-law had freed up for him, but he contracted hepatitis, which eventually claimed his life. Didn't this bereavement make Big Brother the last member of the Xuan family in the village? As the saying goes, "Emotion moves within and takes shape in words," his lamentations were justifiable expressions of his deep-down resentment.

I concluded from my big brother's grief that he had not been let in on the closely guarded secret of the Xuan family history. He had no idea of his true lineage. His birth mother and Grandpa had never breathed a word about it to anyone. He was no imbecile, but he was no match for his mother and Grandpa in their smartness. Therefore he had not discovered the secret, nor would he ever be able to, because no one will ever tell him the truth. There is simply no need to do so. The world abounds in unraveled mysteries. In the case of Ali Baba's treasure trove, everybody wants to know the incantation that opens the door, but in the case of Pandora's Box, why would anyone want to release the many misfortunes and calamities just to satisfy one's curiosity?

The funeral procession in Grandpa's honor was quite impressive, with eight strongly built men carrying the coffin. Following behind

were more than a hundred neighbors and relatives, led by cadres of the production brigade
and the production team, including, of all
people, the deputy director of the "Four Clean-
Ups Movement" (1963–1966) task force. Father and I brought up the rear. Grandpa died
a timely death. If he had died a few months
later, he would not have received such honor,
because in those pre-Cultural Revolution days,
people at least took the trouble of complying
with state policies. Even proponents of the
theory that "Like begets like," in attacking
people of the wrong class origin, moved down
the family tree rather than up or horizontally. Grandpa had been a "poor peasant," in
the official "class status" nomenclature, as his
forefathers three generations back had been.
The fact that his only son—my father—was
owner of a small carpet factory and therefore
a member of the bourgeoisie, did no harm to
Grandpa's class status. On the contrary, it was
known throughout the village and the production team—in fact, throughout the entire production brigade for tens of miles around—that

the only son of the Xuan family was an unfilial son who had refused to look after his father, abandoned his first wife whom he had married in his humble "chaff and husks" days, and had done nothing for his very own eldest son—my big brother. In their profound sympathy for Grandpa's misfortunes, the villagers showed him tolerance, and thanks to this, as well as the relaxed policies, Grandpa had enjoyed "poor peasant" political status to the last day of his life. And so the mourners progressed en masse to the sunny slope at the eastern end of the village, where only those with the right class background and political status were entitled to have graves. My big brother's birth mother had been laid to rest there a few years earlier.

I had the good sense to trail at the very end of the procession, holding on to Father as I walked along. The way Father kept his head low and his eyes to the ground was quite fitting for someone in his position on such an occasion. I knew that he was hoping desperately for this whole thing to be over quickly, so that he could be out of the place as soon as possible, a place that he had spurned, a place where he, in return, was held in contempt. I remember that early in my childhood, I had heard him mention his home village in passing. The disgusted look on his face as he said the following will never fade from my memory: "Unfruitful hills, unfriendly waters, untamed women, unruly men! Definitely not a place fit for anyone to live in!"

I didn't learn until years later in my study of history that the first eight words were, in fact, what Emperor Qianlong (1736–1795) had said about the region north of the Huai River when passing it during one of his visitations to the south. How my father, a businessman with only a grade school education, had picked up that line is more than I can imagine.

As I walked along, inconspicuously bringing up the rear of the funeral procession, I surveyed my surroundings and ran my eyes over the land that, having nurtured my ancestors, was where the Xuan family's roots lay.

2

My Father and My Grandmother

What stretched before me was an expanse of barren land. Actually, "barren" was an overstatement. There was something growing in the yellowish soil, although the sparse, trembling and ripening wheat stalks were so thin and their ears so small that the soil was exposed to view and, seen from afar, appeared to be bare of any crops. Only when one drew close would the plants in their sorry condition become visible. The hardened soil was covered with a layer of yellow dust that whirled about with the slightest puff of wind. Only the tufts of weeds by the roadside gave some life to the place that was otherwise devoid of greenery.

There were no rivers, ditches, or canals, only some pits that, before the last winter and spring, had once held water. But now, the yellow earth on the bottom of the pits was so parched that the crisscross cracks looked like the lines on a chessboard. Some of the wider ones reminded me of Big Brother's gaping mouth as he wailed when Grandpa's body was being lowered into the coffin. There were no trees. Almost all the trees in the region had been felled in 1958. The few that survived the massive logging campaign came to grief two years later: The bark was peeled off to fill stomachs and the timber fed the flames of the kitchen fires. There were no mountains, either. All that met the eyes were low hills denuded of vegetation. This was the most impoverished region in Anhui Province, with no distinctive attributes that mark it out from other places. Located in between the celebrated Yellow Mountain and the flat Wuhu region, it was shorn of all favorable feng shui features. The hillocks, without even a rock, were covered with a layer of dry, powdery loess. Looking into the distance, I was able to make out some clusters of houses. So we were approaching a village. The uniform yellow earthen walls and thatched roofs were just as diminutive and dismal-looking as the wheat stalks in the fields.

Turning my eyes to my father, I was struck by a sense of how he looked a misfit in this place where he had been born and raised. Even while he was trailing behind, staring at his toes, he still kept an erect posture, unlike the villagers who seemed to be always carrying heavy burdens on their bent shoulders, and his face remained clean shaven. He had been holding on to his habit of shaving his face with a Double Arrow razor first thing in the morning since his arrival here a few days earlier for the funeral, and this set him apart from his clansmen with their dark stubble. Father's shirt collar was snowy white, because he had only this morning put on a clean shirt that my mother had stuffed in his bag, out of respect for his father's funeral. But this dazzling whiteness further accentuated the fact that he was at odds with his surroundings. His zippered jacket was

even more eye-catching. It was neither a Mao
suit nor a tunic made of homespun cloth, nor
a traditional jacket buttoned down the front.
No! It was a zippered jacket of dark gray tweed
with light gray fake fur around the collar and
the cuffs. You know, Xiangzhu, that nowadays
there's nothing out of the ordinary about such
a jacket. In fact it's quite old-fashioned. But
in that place and at that time, it was enough to
make Father as conspicuous as a drop of oil in
water. It was small wonder that when we were
passing several small villages, it was invariably
the very tail end of the grand procession that
threw the spectators in front of the thatched
huts into flutters of excitement. As they pointed
at my father, jabbering away, their emaciated
dogs also found themselves attracted to him
and trotted behind him for a good part of the
way, barking furiously.

For quite some time, I was mystified by how
Father had managed to extricate himself from
such surroundings and become a completely
different person. After I returned home from
the funeral, I set about pumping my mother,

my eldest sister, and sometimes, my father himself for information in an attempt to get to the bottom of the mystery. But after I succeeded in establishing all the facts, I found the story pretty mundane. To put it bluntly, Father left his home village "to flee an arranged marriage."

When Father was fourteen, my grandparents had an important but by no means heated debate.

"Tell me! What do you have against that girl Peach?"

"I never said I had anything against the girl. She's not bad at all."

"Then why do you refuse to let my son marry her? You must be planning to wait until I work myself to death through farming and housework, so that you can then get yourself a young and pretty one, right?"

"Keep your voice down! Aren't you afraid the neighbors will laugh? I was just saying …"

"Whatever you say doesn't mean a thing! I'll hold the wedding for them once autumn is over and before the New Year. Hey! What's so bad about becoming a mother-in-law this year and a grandmother next year?"

"Zhigao is only fourteen. He doesn't know anything."

"He doesn't? How come you did when you were fourteen? You knew how to get on my ..."

"Enough! But that was because you taught me ..."

"Well, that settles it, then! Peach is nineteen, as I was. Won't she be able to teach my little Zhigao a thing or two? If Zhigao can do well in school, why shouldn't he be up to that job?"

"Well, the girl has scruples ..."

"What crap! Who doesn't have scruples? Tell me! Now listen to me: After Zhigao marries her, don't you dare try anything with her!"

My grandmother was a holy terror with a fearsome reputation throughout the village and beyond. She was not a native of those parts but had gone to the Xuan Family Village at age nineteen with her mother in their flight from famine. After her mother died in the temple to the local tutelary god, she was taken into our family as a child bride for my grandfather who was then not yet thirteen. By all accounts, she wasn't a holy terror at the time. In fact, she was gentle and quiet and smiled at everyone she saw, showing her two dimples. Unexpectedly, a plague spread around the village less than a year later and claimed the lives of nearly half the village population within a few days. My great grandparents also perished, but before she died, my great grandmother officiated at my grandfather's wedding. After the groom and the bride made the nuptial bows to heaven and earth and to her, she immediately forced them to consummate their marriage in the small room in the west wing of the thatched hut while she herself, tenaciously gasping for breath, lay in waiting on a wooden door panel that had been put on the floor of the main hall. It was not until Grandma went up to her with a flaming red face and a hung head and said, "It's been done," that the old lady gave up the ghost. From that moment on, Grandmother began to develop into a shrew. If she hadn't learned to be tough, she would not have been able to keep in line her little husband with his quietly mischievous ways, or to get the upper hand over those shameless ruffians who kept scaling the wall to peek at her when she was in the outhouse. If she hadn't learned to be tough, even the chickens and ducks of the richer families and the emaciated dogs of the poor would have trampled upon her and her little husband. She became the main pillar of the Xuan family, looking after her husband who was too young to know much, and tilling the two *mu* [a Chinese Unit, one *mu* equals about 667 sq.m] of hillside land inherited from the Xuan ancestors. Even though the land was on a sunny slope, the soil could not have been leaner. Only wheat and corn could grow there, yielding enough for their subsistence. Seeds of all other varieties of crops were sowed in vain.

Grandma was overworked. She had conceived four times but Father was the only child that survived. Her love for my father far exceeded what an average farming family could afford: My father finished grade school and, by age thirteen or fourteen, had never really

worked in the fields. Her love for him peaked
when he had just had his fourteenth birthday.
As if by a magic trick, Grandma took home,
from a place even poorer than the Xuan Family
Village, an eighteen-or-nineteen old girl called
Peach as a bride for my father Xuan Zhigao,
in exchange for one sack of corn dregs. After
a discussion with my grandfather, or rather a
monologue in which Grandpa could hardly
get a word in edgewise, she drove the nineteen-
year-old Peach and her fourteen-year-old son
into the newly decked-out small room at the
western end of the house, just as her mother-
in-law had done to her and her husband.

Unlike my great grandmother who was
bursting with impatience on her deathbed,
my grandmother was in no hurry. She
waited until broad daylight the next morning
before she went to knock on the door of the
western room, to learn what had transpired.
Surprisingly, the door yielded upon her first
rap, and there, what should she see but her
precious son lying on the mud floor, wrapped
up in a brand new quilt, and her daughter-in-

law, sitting all curled up in a corner of the bed, fully clad! Her head sunk low, she appeared to be sound asleep.

Grandma grabbed a broom and rained blows down on her daughter-in-law.

"You certainly know how to get a good night's sleep!" She yelled. "You certainly know how to live an easy life! Who do you think you are? A lady of the first rank? The Emperor's Number-One Consort?"

As the blows of the broom continued, each accompanied by a string of curses, the bride was convulsed with silent weeping. Upon hearing the commotion, Grandpa rushed over to see what was happening but he could do no more than rub his hands and pace in circles at the door, all the while muttering, "Oh stop it! Stop it! This is too much! Too much!" He never dared enter his daughter-in-law's bridal chamber.

My father, snugly asleep on the floor, finally woke up with a start. Looking bewildered when he first sat up, he then listened and watched for a few moments, and, naturally, his memory came back to him. All of a sudden, he jumped up, charged at my grandmother, wrested the broom from her, and flung it savagely to one corner of the room.

Mother and son glared ferociously at each other, like two fighting bulls.

At fourteen, Father was big and tall for his age, and was half a head taller than my strongly built grandmother. Far from "not knowing anything," as my grandfather put it, he, in fact, knew everything there was to know. As the little scholar of the village, he was not going to let his mother run his life the way his grandmother had run his father's. He wouldn't even so much as cast a glance at the girl who had been presented to him in exchange for a sack of corn dregs. As it happened, though, he may not have looked her full in the face, but she had nevertheless entered his line of vision, and he found this Peach more like a small dried-up date, looking not much younger than his mother. After Grandma had driven him into the western room, he retrieved a straw mat from under the bed, took a new quilt from the bed, and made himself a shakedown on the floor—all done as if the other person in the room did not exist. He was not upset because he had already worked out a plan. After having rightly surmised that his mother was going to arrange a marriage for him, he had asked a teacher in his school to introduce him to a shop in Nanjing, capital of Jiangsu Province, to begin an apprenticeship, and was therefore ready to do a disappearing act. Quickly he fell sound asleep, totally oblivious to the dried and puckered "date" cowering in one corner of the bed.

Grandma's torment of the thin "date" in his presence was more than he could bear.

"I chose to sleep on the floor!" he said. "This had nothing to do with her. Why beat her? You're just making her take the rap for me!"

Grandma jumped. "You brat! Just as they say, a married man forgets his mother. You chose to sleep on the floor because you didn't know any better, but she's so much older than you are. How can she not know anything?

Couldn't she have carried you to bed and warmed your feet?"

My father turned on his heels and took off. As he bumped into my grandfather at the door, he had the effrontery to spit at the old man. He had exactly my grandmother's temperament. Both of them terrorized my faint-hearted grandfather. Without bothering to notify anyone, Father took along a few articles of clothing and started out on his southbound journey.

3

My Father and Second Auntie

Once gone, Father stayed away for six whole years.

I have no intention of going into detail about how a Chinese businessman with no foreign capital made his fortune. Since I'm telling you the secrets of the Xuan family tonight, Xiangzhu, I should keep my story focused. I'm going to skip all the particulars about how my father had gone from a cotton-fluffing store in Nanjing to a wool-cleaning workshop in Zhenjiang and then to a wool mill on the outskirts of Suzhou, or about how he moved up from an apprentice to a skilled hand, and then an appraiser of wool purity. Let me come to 1931, the year that saw the start of the war of Japanese aggression in Northeast China. Twenty years old now, my father triumphantly marched from the outskirts of Suzhou to the city proper and rented a huge but dilapidated one-story building on Quanfu [Complete Happiness] Road by Chang Gate and, after some minor renovations, his factory went into operation under the impressive name of "Zhenhua [Rejuvenate China] Carpet Factory," which was inscribed proudly on the placard hanging by the gate. In fact, there was only one antiquated wool-fluffing machine and one foot-activated, manually-operated carpet weaving machine in the otherwise empty premises. As soon as the wool-fluffing machine was plugged in, it began to screech and rumble and, amid the deafening noise, the fluffed wool flew all about, only half of which landed in the wool storage bins. Luckily, even though the building was in sad need of repair, the walls were at least intact and the roof was still there, so the wool drifting in the air eventually settled down on the floor rather than outside the building for the benefit of other people. After the machine was turned off, a big broom could sweep up a good full catty of wool. As for that carpet weaver, it was no more than an enlarged version of the common hand-operated loom used by rural women. The only difference was in the material.

Actually there is more to tell about that carpet weaver: I once worked on it! It was in 1955 or thereabouts. I went to Suzhou to ask Father for tuition and I found my way to Zhenhua Carpet Factory. Father let me try my hand at the machine. It had a long wooden block under it, not unlike the pedals of a piano. The moment I stepped on it, the warp threads on the loom separated into two parallel rows, with the odd-numbered warp threads on top and the even-numbered ones down below, allowing just enough room in the middle for the shuttle to go through. The shuttle had colored yarn attached to it. With each movement of the hand, the shuttle swept with a whoosh from right to left horizontally, thus filling the space with the yarn. I remember that there was a brush in front of the machine that ran the whole length of the loom. After stepping on the pedal with one's right foot and moving the shuttle with one's right hand, one would hold the brush with the left hand and move it toward one's chest, and the yarn that had just filled the space between the warp would be tightly held in place, thus completing one step in the weaving process.

Yes, basically, everything was done manually, which was why, in 1956, during the socialist reform campaign to convert private ownership of enterprises to joint state-private ownership, the policy-makers debated among themselves long and hard about whether to put my father into the category of "capitalist" or "small proprietor of a handicraft workshop." Contrary to Father's wish to make the latter list, he ended up as a "capitalist," the main justification being: First, his capital exceeded the cut-off line of twenty million in the old currency, and second, he had two regular employees—the account keeper and the operator of the carpet-weaving machine. In spite of the fact that the account keeper was my father's brother-in-law and the weaver was an uncle of my father's, also bearing the surname of Xuan, class differences outweighed ties of kinship. Since hiring people meant exploitation, my father became a "capitalist."

But I digress. Let me come back to the secret of the Xuan clan. So, with due pomp and circumstance, Father founded Zhenhua Carpet Factory with its nonstop earsplitting rumbles. Soon thereafter, he fell in love.

The second daughter of the general store opposite West Garden at the northern end of Quanfu Road took a fancy to him.

It was not a large store but, because of its proximity to a major tourist attraction, the owner had a never-ending supply of clients throughout the four seasons of the year, and business was better than some of the stores downtown. Since wealth begets hubris, as they say, Mr. Wen, the owner, had acquired the status of a local despot. Some of the local riffraff addressed him respectfully as "Master Wen" and worked in collusion during the day to help him coax tourists into buying incense sachets, rosary beads, and clay Buddha figurines for more than they were worth and, in the evenings, they gathered in the back room of the store to play dice and mah-jong, for the Wen family residence had become a de facto gambling house on Quanfu Road.

Father's rental of that one-story structure and display of the placard that proudly bore the factory's name had the unintended consequence of stealing a good part of the Wen family's glory. The reason is simple. As I've said before, Father's factory boasted two machines—a mechanized device for wool-fluffing and a manually-operated loom for carpet weaving. At the beginning, Father did both jobs himself without hiring a single worker. However, as can be easily imagined by anyone without even the slightest knowledge of carpet weaving, there were at least two procedures between wool-fluffing and carpet-weaving that could not be accomplished by my father alone in that large empty building. First, the wool must be spun into yarn; second, the white yarn must be dyed before it could be woven on the loom. Father's factory had the mere appearance of a regular factory, thanks to the magnificent plate by the gate. In reality, these two major procedures were quite beyond him, and the assembly line was nonexistent. But, as I have said before, Father's high IQ makes up for what he lacks in educational attainment. He had done his homework before selecting the location for his factory. Quanfu Road on the outskirts of the city, being somewhere between the city proper and the rural areas, was neither too urbanized nor too rustic for his purpose. Most residents along both sides of this long block, apart from a few shop owners, were members of the urban poor without jobs or regular incomes. Some supported their families by doing backbreaking labor like pulling carts. Some managed to live from hand to mouth by doing odd jobs for candy stores in the city, like de-shelling walnuts and melon-seeds. Some eked out a living by collecting garbage in the city, carrying baskets on their backs. With an eye on the cheap labor to be had on this block, my father, while having the two cumbersome machines transported to the one-story building, also had a carpenter make about a dozen small identical spinning wheels to turn wool into yarn. Then he asked an old woman, who was something of a local hiring agent, a matchmaker, and a pimp rolled into one, to scour the block for women skilled in needlework and to tell them to go to Zhenhua for jobs making yarn. Those without spinning wheels at home could use the factory-owned equipment, but the cost would later be deducted in installments from their wages.

Soon more than twenty households became Zhenhua's off-site mini-workshops. After the buzzing spinning wheels produced balls of yarn, the women delivered them to the crumbling factory building in exchange for a couple of banknotes, making no less than their men who pulled rickshaws and carried bulky sacks all day long under the blazing sun or driving rain. All and sundry, men and women, began to call the man from Anhui "Boss Xuan"—the man covered all over with wool from the thunderous wool-fluffing machine.

So, Boss Xuan distributed wool, took in yarn, hired a neighbor to deliver the yarn to a dye house on Stone Street in the city, and before long, hauled back a cartful of colorful yarn. Boss Xuan then personally stepped onto the carpet-weaver and, with movements of his hands and feet, colorful carpets with simple but pretty patterns materialized. As the days and months went by, they gathered to a pile. And then merchants descended on the factory to check them out, carts came to transport the merchandise, and Boss Xuan hired bricklayers to renovate the factory building. One sunny corner of the building was converted into a small bedroom with a plastered ceiling and it began to be filled up with quite decent-looking pieces of furniture, such as a wooden bedframe strung with crisscross coir ropes, a desk, and a chair.

To begin with, this man from Anhui covered with fluffy wool did not arrest the attention of Master Wen who lived opposite West Garden. But one fine day, when Master Wen was walking down Quanfu Road in the

direction of the teahouse on Stone Street,
rubbing two iron balls in his hand, he ran into
three or four acquaintances who, parcels of
pale yellowish yarn under their arms, hurried
past him without stopping except to give him a
nod or an awkward smile by way of a greeting.
Master Wen immediately caught on to the fact
that Boss Xuan had stolen away a good portion
of his power and influence. He was seized with
rage. That very evening, he told a few ruffians
to go to Zhenhua and "raise a rumpus." As for
what exactly they were supposed to do, he said,
"It's up to you," meaning they could give free
play to their considerable imaginations.

"Just show him who the real boss is around
here," he continued. "Let him know that
Quanfu Road is not his kingdom. He'd better
take along his bedding and get out!"

"Come back!" An order sharply delivered
from behind Master Wen brought the lackeys
to an abrupt halt. "Have you so stuffed
yourselves that you have nothing better to do
than find a way to die? Come back into the
house and get on with your gambling games!"

The owner of that high-pitched and crisp voice was Master Wen's second daughter, the cherished lustrous pearl in his palm, doubling as mistress of the house. Mrs. Wen had developed Parkinson's disease quite early on. Believing that the Buddha could cure her ailment in this life or exempt her from the torment of her shaking in her next reincarnation, she spent the better part of each day offering incense at prayer services in the temples. For a good number of years now, Miss Wen Xiuzhu had been the sole supervisor of the Wen household's affairs. Under her gentle and mild exterior, Miss Wen had a steely character. When she spoke, the softness of her tone belied the steel in her words. She was not only a shrewd housekeeper, but also a born diplomat with considerable business acumen. As a result even Master Wen regularly deferred to her, to some extent. Now that she had spoken up, no one dared defy her. Besides, they were only too glad to have some fun rather than get themselves in trouble. With a guilty glance at Master Wen, the men quickly retreated to the gambling room.

Before Master Wen could say a word, Miss Wen launched into the following admonition: "Dad! I've always said that you are just like General Zhang Fei, Monk Sagacious Lu, and General Cheng Yaojin in traditional opera— long on valor but short on wit. You do injustice to your surname Wen [Scholarly]! Why don't you change it to Wu [Military]?" This little-girl act that she put on certainly had a soothing effect on Master Wen's temper.

"Now listen," she went on. "Boss Xuan of Zhenhua came just this afternoon with a large red box and asked to see you. There!"

Following the direction of her pouting lips, Master Wen's eyes fell upon a red paper box of refreshments on the table.

"It's not much of a gift," she continued, "but don't turn up your nose at it. At least he showed good intentions. What's most important, he was here to discuss his big plans with you. But where were you? You were away at a teahouse, and Mother had gone to Xuanmiao Temple. So I had to take it upon myself to talk with him.

This is how it went …"

Having knocked about the lower reaches of the Yangtze River for six or seven years, my father knew all too well the power of local despots and had therefore devised well in advance a plan to deal with Master Wen of Quanfu Road. Equipped with the red box, he had gone to Miss Wen at precisely a time when he knew Master Wen was absent. To do him justice, he never plotted to come up in the world through a marriage alliance with Miss Wen. He paid her this visit only because he had learned that Miss Wen was the key figure in the Wen family. In addition, her rosy little cheeks and charming little mouth lent her such a kindly look that he hoped she would be easier to talk to than the old man. To Miss Wen he laid everything out in the open with a Northerner's straightforwardness: "Please ask Master Wen and his subordinates to have the kindness to allow me to operate my factory in this place. In return, when paying the spinners, I will substitute a part of the wages with some daily necessities from the Wen family's store in the form of soap, toilet paper, cooking oil, salt, soy sauce, vinegar, brooms, washboards, fabric, underwear, and whatnot. Consider this a way to help Master Wen build up his business. Also, among Zhenhua's semi-finished yarn, those that are of purer quality and are more nicely spun can be used to knit into ordinary woolen pants or woolen jackets, which I will then sell to you at a price significantly lower than the market wholesale price. I don't care how much you re-sell them for. On festive occasions, I will of course come to pay my respects to Master Wen. Barring other considerations, Master Wen's age, of itself, calls for respect. Miss Wen, please convey my sentiments to your father!"

That was the day on which Miss Wen made up her mind to marry my father. She was a typical Suzhou girl, a little on the plump side, with a round face, smooth skin, arched eyebrows with very little space in between, and slightly slanting, long eyes with single-layer eyelids. Her nose was flat but small and cute, and went very well with her thin-lipped tiny mouth. She felt attracted to my father not only because he was so straightforward and capable of getting things done, but also because she admired his imposing looks of a typical Northerner. Big of frame, he had sharply chiseled features, with protruding brows, a high-bridged nose, and a well-marked, firm mouth. He also sported side-whiskers. This was not a face often seen in the south. Many men in the lower reaches of the Yangtze River have narrow eyes and eyebrows, with either weak jaws or chins that are overly soft and rounded. What's more, they seem to have less hair. Miss Wen was captivated by Father's looks the first time she saw him. As mistress of a merchant's household, she knew the value of a rare commodity. With a disposition like a bamboo strip ubiquitous in the region—sharp-edged and likely to bend but never to crack, she was not one to be easily shaken in her resolve. Eventually she succeeded in becoming Mrs. Xuan. Being the second daughter in the Wen family, her nephews had always called her "Second Auntie," and so somehow, after marriage, she became known to all and sundry as "Second Auntie." As I see it, this term of address is predetermined by divine will. Didn't my father have a number-one wife Peach in his home village? Wasn't "Second Auntie" a hint to Miss Wen's status as a concubine?

4

My Father and Auntie Peach

Master Wen exploded with rage as soon as he figured out that his precious daughter was determined to marry that miserable Xuan Zhigao from Anhui. "Don't you know that he has a wife in his home village up north?" he thundered. "You cheap hussy! How can you accept the status of a concubine?"

"Father, don't get so worked up! What did he know when he was only fourteen? Don't you see that that country bumpkin would make a perfect wife for his father? She's five or six years older than him!"

"That's none of my business! I only know that that bastard Xuan is married! I'm not

going to let you become a concubine even if I
have to beat you to death and go to jail!"

"All right, go ahead and beat me!" Miss
Wen, later to become Second Auntie of the
Xuan family, threw herself at her father, head
first. "Show me! Beat me to death! If you don't,
you are a bastard!"

Being after all the valiant daughter of a local
despot, Miss Wen, under the daily cultivation of
the riffraff who frequented the Wen residence,
had picked up their way of doing things. And
now, as she applied with a vengeance what she
had learned, Master Wen found himself at a
loss what to do. At his wits' end, he did what a
father in traditional opera or the rulers of those
days would do under similar circumstances: he
locked her up. While keeping her confined in
a room in the back of the house under twenty-
four-hour watch, he pressed ahead with plans
to launch an all-out effort to drive my father
out of Quanfu Road.

At this juncture, a letter from Anhui came
by express mail. My grandmother had died of
a sudden illness and my father was asked to go

back immediately for the funeral.

Father cried his eyes out upon receiving the letter. Now that his mother had died, he recalled her many kindnesses and came to realize what an unfilial son he had been, for he had not returned to his home village even once in six years. He padlocked the gate of his factory and returned posthaste to his home village.

My grandmother had died of her own fiery temper.

I have said before that the Xuan ancestors had left my grandfather two *mu* of land on a slope. Of lean soil, it managed to yield only one crop of winter wheat and one crop of corn per year. However poor the soil was, it was, after all, still the Xuan family's possession and, after my father's departure, the three-member family depended on the yield of the two-*mu* land for survival. So, throughout the four seasons of the year, the three of them kept themselves busy working on the yellow and hardened earth. During his six year absence, my father wrote a few letters home in the first three years just to tell them that he was okay, and, in the last three years, had only sent some money on festive occasions, although not enough to buy more than a few lengths of fabric to cover the more delicate parts of the body. Even so, my grandparents were puffed up with pride and showed every person they met my father's letters and the scanty articles of clothing made with the fabric that my father had paid for. Those served as evidence that their son had made his mark in the world and, in addition, was a filial son and a devoted husband. For questions as to why he had never paid a visit home, my grandmother had a ready answer. Resolutely she said, "Xue Pinggui [of the Tang dynasty] didn't return to his home village in eighteen years until he became a high official, and the Great Yu [founder of the Xia dynasty] was so busy with his water control project that he had passed his own house three times without entering. How can men who do great things be tied down by their own little cozy nests?"

However, when things were not going

her way, or when she was exhausted from backbreaking labor, she would unleash her temper on Peach. "You useless thing!" she would say. "If you hadn't been such an eyesore, if you had been able to win his heart, wouldn't my son have returned home, if only once, in all these years? The Xuan family got you and lost a son. You are a jinx, a white tiger spirit, every inch of you!"

Auntie Peach was a woman of few words. She never talked back, and never did more than try her best to hold back the tears that welled in her eyes. My grandfather, in the meantime, would heave one sigh after another off to one side, as if to say he also sorely missed his son, or to express his deep sympathy for his daughter-in-aw. Usually, his sighs would come to an abrupt halt as soon as Grandma stopped her verbal assault from sheer physical exhaustion.

Early in the summer of 1931, due to unfavorable weather conditions, the two-*mu* field of the Xuan family yielded only about two hundred catties of wheat, a 40% reduction

from previous years. After doing the math
and realizing that even if supplemented by
bran, what little they had harvested could not
last them until winter, she grew desperate.
Without waiting for a soaking rain so that the
soil could be loosened somewhat, she busily
led my grandfather and Peach in plowing the
field, hoping that by sowing the corn, the next
crop, earlier and more densely than usual, they
might be able to harvest a few more piculs
of corn to make up for the loss in wheat. As
usual, she had Grandpa hold the handles
while she herself and Peach pulled the plow
in front with a thick rope over their backs. In
fact, they were doing what was supposed to
be done by oxen, because the Xuan family did
not own an ox. Day and night they turned the
sun-hardened yellow earth. After a few days,
all three of them found their strength leaving
them but my grandmother, with confidence
in her own tough constitution, continued to
work nonstop, all the while yelling, "Peach, you
lazybones! Pull harder! How dare you loaf on
the job! I can see that your rope is slackening.

Do you want to work me to death? Hey! The one in the back! Push harder! Do you expect the two of us women to support you for the rest of your life?"

As it turned out, she tripped over a clod of earth and fell sideways onto the field. No one had anticipated her fall. Peach, loyally doing her mother-in-law's bidding, kept pulling the rope for all she was worth, her head bent low. My grandfather, with his wife's sharp rebukes still echoing in his ears, kept pushing the plow forward with might and main. All of a sudden, the plowshare ran over my grandmother's body, leaving a long, deep, gaping wound. As blood spurted, Grandma gave a grunt—from fatigue or from pain I can't tell for sure—and, her eyeballs rolling straight up, she passed out.

Peach froze with fright and remained bent low with the thick rope over her back, as if she were still the plowing ox. With the presence of mind of a man, my grandfather quickly regained his wits. He grabbed a handful of soil and spread it on Grandma's wound. Blood

quickly soaked through the soil. He kept
adding more soil to the wound, as if to stop the
flow of water as it breached a dyke. Soon the
wound was filled up with yellow soil and, of
course, soon thereafter, Grandma began to run
a fever. Three days later, she was carried onto
a door panel that had been laid on the floor of
the main hall, and there she breathed her last.

Throughout these three days she did not
hurl accusations at anyone but lay quietly,
muttering "Zhigao, Zhigao." During a brief
recovery of consciousness before she drew
her last breath, she looked up at Peach, who
was standing by with her head sunk low, and,
enunciating each word crisply, gave these
instructions: "Go to bed with Zhigao, like the
wife you are! You teach him!"

Peach threw herself on Grandma and
wailed with deeper grief than she would have
done for her own mother.

Father hurried back for the funeral. He
spared no expense to make the funeral as
grand an affair as possible. Indeed, the funeral
deeply convinced all the villagers that this

scion of the Xuan family had truly come up in the world. One detail alone was enough to illustrate this point: He wore an ankle-length gown. Another detail: The snow-white collar of a silk shirt peeped out of the top of his gown. A third detail: The coffin he had bought for his mother was made of thick boards of timber painted with black varnish. Moreover, he hired a band of musicians for a prayer service—something unprecedented in the Xuan Family Village which boasted no real rich man. Villagers unanimously agreed that the departed Mrs. Xuan had been telling the truth. Her son had indeed struck it rich.

The very evening after the burial, Grandpa relayed to Father the dying wishes of Grandma, and disappeared into his own tiny room in the eastern wing of the house.

My father sat glumly in the main hall, smoking nonstop, while Peach went in and out, her head sunk low, cleaning up the mess in the main hall. Then she carried a chamber pot into Grandpa's room and, as she was heading for her own tiny room in the western wing, a

small oil lamp in hand, Father raised his head
and called out after her, "Peach!"

This was the first time Father called her by
her name. Peach gave such a violent start that
her oil lamp almost fell on the floor.

Still thin and small, Peach was twenty-six
but looked much younger than her age partly
because her light cotton blouse concealed her
figure that had been well-developed from all
the years of farming and partly because of the
dim light that the oil lamp cast on her face.
Being inexperienced and of a shy and quiet
nature, she trembled all over upon hearing
my father call her. Of course, in that instant,
she also recalled Grandma's order "You teach
him."

At the sight of Peach on the verge of tears
in her consternation, Father felt a rush of
sympathy, gratitude, tenderness, and guilt. The
memory of Grandma beating her after she and
my father slept apart on their wedding night
now came back to him. He also imagined what
hardships she had to go through day in and
day out during those six long years, tilling the

unfriendly soil and putting up with Grandma's tyranny. Perhaps guided by Grandma's soul in the other world, Father finally resolved to do his conjugal duty. He stood up, took the lamp from Peach, and led her by her trembling hand into the western room. He certainly needed no lessons from Peach. Grandma had grievously underestimated her son!

5

Second Auntie and Father

During Father's absence, Second Auntie kept threatening to kill herself in the confinement of her boudoir. Clamoring for scissors one moment and for ropes the next, she allowed the entire Wen residence no peace.

Master Wen had planned to take advantage of that rascal Xuan's absence and have his men smash up that run-down factory that the recent renovations had not done much to improve, so that my father would have no roof over his head after he returned. To his dismay, a maidservant named Shen leaked the word out to Second Auntie. Though she could not take a step out of her room, Second Auntie's high-pitched and crisp voice echoed through the Wen residence and even down Quanfu Road through the storefront.

"Old man! How dare you! I can outsmart you! If you smash up Mr. Xuan's factory, I will burn down your store! I mean it! All it takes is a little match to set myself on fire! Just you wait!"

Master Wen never gave the order to act, after all.

Second Auntie was in fact predestined to marry my father. While Father was still away, Master Wen began to anxiously look forward to his return because something had gone terribly wrong. What had happened was that his eldest daughter's husband (Second Auntie's brother-in-law), a journalist with a Shanghai newspaper, had suddenly been arrested by the Shanghai Garrison Headquarters for being, allegedly, a member of the "League of Leftist Writers" and a Communist. This son-in-law's mother was Master Wen's elder sister, and he was therefore both nephew and son-in-law to Master Wen. Soon his eldest daughter and his

sister came in tears to his door and pleaded
that he do something to get the journalist
out of jail as soon as possible. They added
that a good number of Communists had
just been executed in Shanghai and that, the
interrogation process having been dispensed
with, the interval between arrest and execution
was less than one month.

Partly out of considerations of kinship and
partly out of fear that such a close relative
guilty of a political crime would get himself
implicated, Master Wen racked his brains for
a plan to bribe high and low to get his nephew
plus son-in-law out of jail. Again, Shen the
servant informed Miss Wen about the turn of
events, and this was Miss Wen's message to her
father: "Old man! Let me out this instant! I'll
go to Xuan Zhigao for help. I know he can do
something about this."

Master Wen did not believe her, but he was
obliged to give it a try. By this time, my father
had hastened back to Zhenhua Factory.

Second Auntie, with her shrewd brain,
remembered that my father had mentioned

to her a grade-school teacher of his, who had later joined the army and then gone south.   Thereafter, the erstwhile teacher joined the Northern Expedition (1924–1927) and then became some kind of an officer in a headquarters in Shanghai. The exact title and functions of the post eluded her, but the information stuck in her memory. Without waiting for Father to get his breath back after his return, she took it upon herself to buy two train tickets to Shanghai and dragged my father along. He went, partly because he was unable to reject her pleading, partly because he wanted to take this opportunity to ingratiate himself with Master Wen, and partly because, in his ignorance about politics, he had no idea how dangerous being implicated in such a case could be for him if he failed. And so he recklessly marched into the Garrison Headquarters at Hengbang Bridge, Shanghai, like a newborn calf that was not afraid of the tiger. On the strength of the bond between fellow villagers and between former teacher and student, plus the two gold bars produced

from Second Auntie's chest, Master Wen's
son-in-law was, surprisingly enough, released
on bail. In fact, when all is said and done, he
was no more than an amateur writer who had
joined the "Leftist League." If he had indeed
been a member of the Communist Party, such
a casual connection of my father's and two
little gold bars from Second Auntie would by
no means have been enough to do the trick.

So Father did the Wen family a great
service.

After the job was done, the two of them
should, by rights, have lost no time in returning
to Suzhou—on Second Auntie's part, to report
on a mission accomplished and to ask for a
reward, and on my father's part, to take care
of his factory that had been closed for about
two weeks. However, scheming Second Auntie
had a mind of her own and bought two train
tickets for the following day, reserving a room
in a nice, clean inn behind the North Station.
When showing my father to it, she said to him,
lying through her teeth, that it was for his
exclusive use and that she would only sit for

a little while before going to her sister's home nearby to retire for the night. But, once the door was closed after the two of them, she refused to budge, saying that she wanted to marry my father that very evening. She was determined to create a fait accompli and hold the wedding after they returned to Suzhou.

"I have a wife in my village!" said my father. "If you want to marry me, you'll have to be a concubine!"

"I don't mind. I've known about your wife all along. I'm a woman of a practical turn of mind. Since your factory is in Suzhou, you are my husband in reality."

She then went on to lay all her cards on the table, saying that the Wen family, with a sizable income from the gambling house plus the profits from the store over the years, had quite a hefty amount of savings, and that the two gold bars that she had brought along had been only a fraction of the dozens of gold bars in her father's possession. She added that if my father married her, the Wen and Xuan families could join forces in running the factory and put an end to its current sorry state.

"We can buy that entire row of bungalows next to Zhenhua," she continued. "There will be no need to contract spinning jobs out. Let's partition the building into different workshops: a wool-fluffing workshop, a spinning workshop, a dyeing workshop, a carpet-weaving workshop. We'll hire people. If the job is worth doing, it's worth doing properly. What do you say?"

The bright prospects and the alluring blueprint could not but raise a flutter in my father's heart. The funeral had cost him his entire savings. To start all over again would be another up-hill journey. How could he, a businessman, give up on an opportunity to do great things—an opportunity that was there for the taking? And how could he reject a charming Suzhou girl determined to marry him even if she became his concubine? That very night, he made Miss Wen Second Auntie of the Xuan family.

6

Second Auntie and Auntie Peach

Fifteen tables were set out for Miss Wen's wedding, to which almost every family on Quanfu Road was invited. Even though everyone knew my father had a wife in Anhui, none professed any knowledge of it. Little people know what is meant by the saying, "A loose tongue invites trouble." Who would want to have a window smashed one day and a packet of shit tossed into the kitchen the next day by the local ruffians? Every resident on Quanfu Road knew all too clearly that anyone who got on the bad side of the Wens would have no peace. Besides, though Father had only been in the neighborhood for less than a year, he minded his own business and did many favors for his neighbors. Apart from the nuisance of that rumbling wool-fluffing machine, he did not seem to have given them any trouble. People living in small alleys in Suzhou went out of their way to be agreeable, docile, circumspect, and to yield and be kind to others. So, upon receiving the Wen family's wedding invitations, everyone rejoiced and, bearing gifts bought with their meager wages, attended the banquet in the sprawling Wen residence.

Every voice throughout the neighborhood could testify to the sumptuousness of the banquet. Even after more than forty years, those who had attended the banquet still retained vivid memories of the occasion. In 1958, when writing "three histories" was all the rage in the literary circles, a half-illiterate director of security in the Quanfu Road neighborhood committee proposed, in her clouded wits, to include that wedding banquet in the "history of the block." The old lady even recited the menu, swallowing her saliva, to every appearance carried away in her admiration. However, the sober-headed writer took down her account, true to the principle that "Literature should come from life and be elevated above life" made the banquet into a typical example of a capitalist's decadent lifestyle, showing the way he fleeced the villagers. Another few years later, when my father came under political attack, the factory where he worked held a "class struggle exhibition" with my father as the sole object of denunciation. One of the items posted on the wall was the menu at the wedding banquet, copied in beautiful calligraphy. It was the very menu that the director of security, one of the guests, knew by heart. After passing from hand to hand, the menu eventually came into my possession, an abbreviated version of which is as follows:

Butterfly Cold Dishes (Sixteen cold dishes placed in the middle of the table in the shape of a butterfly)

A Hundred Blossoms (Eighteen saucers containing hors d'oeuvres, placed in a riot of color around the "butterfly")

Stir-fries:

Jade Pieces in Palace Lanterns (Sautéed de-shelled shrimps served on palace-lantern shaped plates)

Two Lovers (Two juxtaposed Wuchang fish)

Illustrious Pearls on the Palm (Fresh green peas with duck feet)

Water lilies with Dates and Sea Cucumber (Sliced chicken in white sauce braised with bright red dates and black sea cucumbers)

Double-Happiness Tendons (Pig tendons sautéed with deep-fried and then water-saturated yellow croaker maw)

Entrées: Crisp-fried duck, chicken in cream sauce, mandarin fish in the shape of a squirrel, soft-shelled turtle stuffed with eight treasures, etc.

Dim Sum: Dual-colored steamed dumplings (some with sweet filling), date sponge cakes (Steamed sponge cakes decorated with dates), A Hundred-Years-of-Conjugal-Bliss pastry (Pastry with a lily-bulb filling of medicinal value), Lucky dumplings (Sticky-rice sweet dumplings with slices of orange)

I had done a careful analysis of the menu. Judging from the menu alone, I could only conclude that form weighed more than

content as far as that wedding was concerned.
In Suzhou, the food capital with its abundance
of restaurants and master chefs, where every
delicacy of land, sea and sky, except the stars
and the moon, could be served on the table
to please the palate, the menu cited above
was nothing more than mediocre. However,
if you read the menu aloud a few times, you
will realize that its designer had taken as great
pains with it as poets with their verses that are
meant to be read out loud. The name of almost
every course came tripping off the tongue, and
was a homophone of a brief phrase expressing
good wishes. For example, "Butterfly" was
a homophone for "invincible." Applied to
Zhenhua, it was a wish for the factory to be
invincible in the business world and to sweep
away all obstacles on its way up. Applied to
Second Auntie, it was a wish for her to be
invincible and second to none, certainly not to
Peach in Xuan Family Village, Anhui! "Two
Lovers," "Double Happiness" and "A Hundred-
Years-of-Conjugal-Bliss" augmented the
ambience of the occasion, and "Dates" was a

homophone for having sons soon. "Illustrious pearls on the palm," a fancy name for some peas with duck feet, was an instance of Second Auntie blowing her own trumpet.

I checked with Father and he confirmed my speculations. He said, "Yes, Suzhou people like auspicious names for everything. Your Second Auntie had examined and approved the menu and, every time a new course was served, a man hired for the purpose would chant out its name, opera-style, in his feminine, high-pitched voice, which was why the director of security was able to file it away in her memory!"

Second Auntie single-handedly ran her own wedding. Her father paid for all the expenses but she kept all the gifts. Soon after the wedding, she bought herself a glittering diamond ring with the cash gifts. It was after the breakdown of law and order some time later that she took it off her finger and hid it at the bottom of a trunk, so that it would not attract undue attention.

Residents on Quanfu Road never mentioned my father's first wife. To them, she was no more than a name without substance, an abstract idea, an imaginary figure. It was Second Auntie, second daughter of the Wen family and mistress of Zhenhua Carpet Factory, who enjoyed the de facto status of Mrs. Xuan, with a fifteen-table banquet to prove it.

When the wedding banquet in Suzhou was in full swing, Auntie Peach in that impoverished village was vomiting herself into a state nearer death than life. One month into her pregnancy, at age twenty-six, she had begun to develop nausea. She lost all appetite and kept throwing up until what came out was nothing but greenish bile. My poor panic-stricken grandfather was at a loss over what to do. He had never done a father's duty. When my grandmother conceived my father, my grandfather was only fourteen. After the day's farm work was done, he spent his surplus energy on climbing trees to search for bird eggs or digging up wild water chestnuts in the pond. He had absolutely no idea how my grandmother had gotten through the nine-month pregnancy or how a baby had managed to materialize in

her arms above her now deflated abdomen.
All by herself, my grandmother, with her
tough constitution and strong character,
raised my father who inherited her aquiline
nose, acting as both father and mother. By
1931, when Peach was pregnant with my eldest
sister, my grandfather was thirty-five. Though
he was, for a time, clueless and thought that
Peach had suddenly fallen seriously ill, his
natural instincts eventually told him what had
happened. Overwhelmed with mixed feelings
of joy and worry, he hesitated.

Then he took out the few silver dollars
that he had received from my father, who had
produced them after a thorough search of all
his pockets before his departure. Not stinting
on expenses, my grandfather made one trip
after another to the county seat—each trip
was more than thirty *li* one way—and bought
for his daughter-in-law abundant supplies of
sweet, sour, and spicy food. He also took on all
the work that needed to be done in the fields
and planted all the corn, to the last kernel.

Auntie Peach found herself basking in

loving care for the first time in her life. For a few months, she lived the life of a grand lady in the tumbledown hut that stood on the yellow earth. As soon as she felt better, she began to putter about the rooms, fixing everything that had been broken or was not in good order. She also washed and mended all the bed sheets and clothes in the house, now occupied only by the two of them, and made everything look new.

My eldest sister was born on the first day of the Lunar New Year. According to fortunetellers, hers was a horoscope fit for a number-one imperial consort. The labor pains started on New Year's Eve. My grandfather wanted to go to a neighboring village five *li* away to get the midwife, but, gnashing her teeth in pain, Peach stopped him, saying, "Don't trouble her when she's just had her New Year's Eve dinner. Get her tomorrow morning. I can get through it." She was too inexperienced to know that this was something beyond her control. Before long, the pain was too much for her. As her groans through clenched teeth became too heartbreaking to hear, Grandpa again offered to go and get the midwife, but Peach said tearfully, "Don't go! It's too late to go anyway. Quickly help me get up and give me the flour bucket that's under the bed."

"You can't be thinking of kneading flour in such a moment?" said Grandpa.

Finding his words both amusing and annoying at the same time, Peach barked, in the way my grandmother used to, "Just get it for me this instant! I can't hold out anymore!"

When he pulled out the white flour bucket, he saw that a clean piece of cloth had already been laid out in it and under the pad was a thick layer of plant ashes. Before he had time to think, he saw that Peach, with one hand holding him in a tight grip, was savagely pulling down her pants with the other hand. The next moment, she flopped down onto the bucket. Hot blood rushed to his head, and he thought in that instant about fleeing the room. He was illiterate but he knew that certain lines between men and women were not to be crossed. And to make matters worse, he was acutely aware of the fact that he was father-in-law to her. However, Peach's grip on him was so tight that all her ten fingers were digging into the flesh around his waist. Stiffly he stood in front of his daughter-in-law who was sitting on the bucket with her pants down, listening to her moans, that she was doing her best to stifle, and her gasps for breath that sounded like each one would be the last, and watching her sweat dripping onto the sheets. He could not find it in his heart to flee. With his coarse and bony hand, he gently wiped away the sweat from Peach's neck and, with his other hand, supported her under her arm, so that she could find it easier to push. Grateful for the warm tenderness of his one hand and firm support of the other, with one blood-curdling scream Peach fulfilled her destiny as a woman. My eldest sister fell onto the cotton pad that had been spread over a layer of soft plant ashes. Her first cry coincided with the first crows of the village roosters.

The vivid scene described above is a result of my deductions after I gained a thorough knowledge of the Xuan family history and observed the local customs at first hand during the grand procession at Grandpa's funeral, enlivened with a dash of imagination that is well within the bounds of plausibility. In our ancestral village, children are still born in that way, which, to the villagers, is convenient and economical. All I need to add is that standing in front of the bucket to lend support to the expectant mother cannot be any other male but the husband. My grandfather was an exception.

7

My Grandfather and My Father

My father didn't want his home villagers to
know that he had set up another family in
Suzhou. An emperor was entitled to a harem
in all his power and glory, but common folks
despise those men who abandon the wives
they married in their humbler days and get
themselves new wives as soon as they've risen
in status. Thanks to the distance between his
home village and Suzhou, Father managed to
keep Grandpa and Auntie Peach in the dark
for two long years. However, as the saying
goes, "No wall can stop the air from getting
through." A villager who had happened to
travel to Suzhou on business knocked at my

grandfather's door first thing in the morning after his return. He pulled my grandfather to a discreet spot beyond the fence and told him, "Your son has got himself a concubine."

"What! This can't be."

"I saw her with my own eyes. She's fat and ugly. Our Peach is much prettier. And that one is a holy terror, too. Your son is a pushover."

"How is that possible?"

"Why not? It's the thing to do for city folks down south. As soon as the men lay their hands on some money, they get themselves one concubine after another. Well, I certainly got to see something of the world this time! So, how are Peach and her daughter?"

"Ah, brother, please do not tell her a word about this!"

"Tell Peach? Of course not! Am I the kind of scoundrel who gloats over other people's sorrows?"

However, in a matter of days, Auntie Peach learned all the accurate details from a woman when both were drawing water by the pond.

By the time Peach arrived home, staggering

every step of the way, only half of the water remained in her buckets. My grandfather, chopping firewood in the yard, knew just from the look on her face that the secret was out. He flung down his ax, rushed to her and reached out a hand for the pole across her shoulder. He meant to help her with the load, but he inadvertently pushed her, and both she and her load of water fell tumbling to the ground.

In the evening, Grandpa entered Peach's room, hoping to cheer her up. "Don't take it too hard, all right? Whatever happens, you remain a member of the Xuan family. You see, you married into this family legitimately and properly, through the services of a matchmaker. Even if he gets himself eight or ten women outside, they are, well, they are concubines, all of them. You are the only legitimate, proper wife. Do you understand? There, there, stop crying, Peach. I feel bad enough. Whatever he says, you are my only daughter-in-law. Come on, Peach …"

Grandpa was a meek and softhearted man, with far less strength of character than my grandmother. At the sight of Peach awash with tears but silent, without a word of complaint, like a frostbitten autumn leaf, my poor grandfather broke down like an old woman in a violent fit of sobbing.

While the two oldest members of the family were crying, my eldest sister, one year old at the time, was fast asleep. She had no idea how long my grandfather and Peach had been crying in the same room, but ever since that day, each time she woke up earlier than usual, if she put out a hand, she could feel my grandfather's stubbles and be tickled into shrieks of laughter. Because she did not leave her home village until she was nine years old, to join Father and Second Auntie in Suzhou, my suspicions are that of us ten siblings, she and I are the only two who were in possession of the top secret of the Xuan family. She had my father's aquiline nose but a higher IQ than his, and at nine years of age, she should have understood something of the world and begun to remember things.

Before Big Sister was three years old, Peach

found herself pregnant again, but not before her figure had begun to show it. Her pregnancy symptoms this time were a large appetite and deep, restful sleep. In two to three months' time, she had filled out and gained a healthy glow in her smooth cheeks and a sparkle in her eyes. Rather than vomiting violently as she had done in her last pregnancy, she did not feel the slightest queasiness. She had made the mistake of putting too much trust in her experience as well as in the old saying, "Breast-feeding keeps pregnancy away." By the time my eldest brother began to move about in her belly, it dawned on her that things had taken a wrong turn.

My grandfather and Auntie Peach discussed the matter in the western room.

"What are we going to do? What are we going to do?" My grandfather kept repeating in the beginning.

Peach, the calmer of the two, said, "I've heard that there is a doctor in Chengguan Town near the county seat, who prescribes abortion medicine."

"That won't do! I've heard that quite a few women have died because of his potent medicine."

"Not all of them have."

"No! That's out of the question." My grandfather could be decisive enough at a critical moment. I'm not going to let you gamble with your life. You must not be impulsive, Peach."

"So, what are we going to do? " It was now Peach's turn to repeat the line.

"Give birth to the baby," said Grandpa. "I want the baby."

"How can I do that? People will ask where the baby came from. Oh, no!" Peach burst into tears.

"Don't worry. I've got an idea." Grandpa grew fearless in the hour of danger.

He took a thirty-*li* trip to the county seat and asked a fortuneteller to write up a letter, which he then sent by express mail to Suzhou. The letter contained only a few brief words: "Father critically ill. Be sure to return immediately."

Father had not returned to his home village in quite a number of years, but he did not want to be called an unfilial son. Since my grandmother had died so suddenly, he thought that the same thing might be happening to my grandfather. After handing over the daily operations of the factory to Second Auntie, he raced off to the train station. Then he switched to bus, after which he covered thirty *li* on foot before he arrived at the Xuan Family Village. Upon throwing open the door, who should he see but his father, in perfectly good condition, squatted on the floor, repairing the basket that was used to collect dog droppings! My eldest sister was also there, standing between my grandfather's knees.

Grandpa spoke up first, to pre-empt my father. "If I hadn't done this, would you have come back? Your daughter is getting big and she hasn't seen you even once." Turning to the girl, he continued, "Go greet your father! You two don't even know each other!"

At the time, my father had no clue as to the motive hidden deep behind what he thought was a practical joke. He got angry but there was nothing he could do. During the last few years he had been racking his brains over a plan to expand his factory. To translate into reality the blueprint that Second Auntie had set out before him was by no means an easy job. The Wen family fortunes may have been quite ample, but as long as Old Mr. Wen was alive, Second Auntie could not make all the financial decisions for the family. Although cheap but good labor was to be easily had on the local market, Quanfu Road produced no wool.

Wool had to be bought from Henan, Shanxi, and Shandong up north. With the Japanese quickly sweeping south after occupying the three Northeastern provinces, these wool-producing provinces were also ready to fall. Zhenhua Factory was likely to lose its supplies of raw material at any moment. A few days before the "critically ill" notification arrived, Father had just returned to Suzhou from Huzhou, Zhejiang, also a wool-producing area. But Southerners being shrewder than

Northerners, Huzhou merchants, with full knowledge of market prices, asked for much more than my father was willing to pay. So he accomplished nothing on his trip to Huzhou, and the money he had spent on travel had gone down the drain. To his dismay, a fire had broken out in his own backyard, so to speak, and again, he had gone to a lot of expense and effort for nothing—all because of what he thought was a whim on Grandpa's part. And he had also been given a fright, more or less. However upset he was, he could do no more than accept his bad luck. He had arrived at the clay hut in early afternoon. In the evening, when he picked up a fluffy, steamed bun that was singularly white because Peach had added flour to the thoroughly kneaded and leavened dough, he had already decided to go first thing in the morning.

Her head hanging low, Auntie Peach went in and out of the room, looking as if she was afraid of raising her head, but my father found nothing amiss. In fact, to him, she was the kind of person who would not let out a peep even if you hit her repeatedly with a club. He thought that with such a docile wife taking care of the old and the young, he would be relieved of a load from his mind. As for his daughter, a healthy and pretty two-year-old now, with a charming little aquiline nose, he had a mind to take her with him to Suzhou in a few years, because Second Auntie had been barren for almost three years. "She must be a fat hen that lays no eggs," he thought. At this point, he looked a little harder at Peach as she did her chores by the oil lamp, and was surprised to find her round arms and lithe waist more alluring than several years before. His anger earlier in the day quickly evaporated. Now that he had regained his peace of mind, he began to ask his father if he had received the money he had sent home over the last couple of years, how the crops were doing in the fields, and whether they still had only wheat and corn. He was glad to learn that they had added tiles on the roof so that it did not leak anymore. He asked, "Why don't you pull the house down in a year or so and build a new one with brick walls? My factory is not doing well at this moment, but after things get better, I'll send more money back, to build a new house and buy another two *mu* of land, not on a slope, but on fertile, flat land."

Father and son chatted until quite late into the evening before they parted to retire for the night. As was only to be expected, my father went into the western room.

Neither father nor son had said a word about Second Auntie. They didn't have the wish, the interest, the courage, or the inclination to talk about her. Grandpa, in particular, with his dark secret, was in no position to denounce his son.

8

My Father and Auntie Peach

This chapter is entirely fictional. How would I know anything about what happened in the bedroom of my father and Auntie Peach?

By bolting up the door of the western room, my father had shut out everyone from the world that belonged to Peach and him. Ah, no, my eldest sister was in the room. Not yet three, she had no sense as yet, but her presence had a bearing on a very important detail in the story I'm going to relate, which is why I must bring this point up in advance.

With regard to what my father and Auntie Peach did, said, and thought during the very last night they spent together in their lives, I have worked out three scenarios:

1. With a yawn, my father entered the room and, without giving any thought to it, bolted the door. Peach gave a start. My eldest sister, not yet asleep, was so frightened at the sight of Father that she hung tightly to Peach's bosom and said, "Mom! Where's my grand ..."

Before she was able to finish, Peach pressed her bosom against the girl's mouth to silence her. Once she got her breath back, my sister began to wail. Feeling sleepy and vexed, my father said with a wave of his hand, "Quiet her down. I'll have to hit the road tomorrow."

Peach heaved an inaudible sigh from relief rather than from grief. She put the girl on the floor and hastened to spread out Father's quilt, which was just narrow enough to accommodate him, and him alone. He quickly crawled under the quilt. Peach carried my sister in her arms and softly paced around the room, all the while patting her and humming a lullaby that soon put both father and daughter to sleep. The next morning, the moment my father opened his eyes, he saw what Peach had packed for his journey: warm white steamed buns and boiled eggs. My sister was still in blissful sleep by his side.

2. My father entered the western room and bolted the door. My sister was already asleep. Peach was sitting by the bedside oil lamp, stitching the sole of a cloth shoe. With a yawn, Father said, "Lie down and sleep now. I'll have to hit the road early tomorrow morning."

Without raising her head, Peach said, "You go to sleep. I'm not sleepy. Let me work a little longer."

Father was slightly disappointed but did not insist. When undressing himself, he threw a few glances at Peach out of the corner of his eye. Because of the proximity, he could make out the wrinkles on her face even though her cheeks had filled out a little. He also saw that her hand holding the needle and thread had short, thick fingers and coarse skin. He recalled Second Auntie's lustrous, smooth skin and small plump hands with five dimples. Then his thoughts went back to the recent stroke that Master Wen had suffered. With Old Wen's face

drooping and looking lopsided, Second Auntie
had taken over the management of the general
store. Now that the merger of the Wen family
business and the Xuan establishment was just
around the corner, he thought of a multitude
of things that needed to be done at Zhenhua.
The excitement he had felt upon arriving had
all vanished. Lying under the quilt, he was no
match for Peach sitting by the lamp. He drifted
off to sleep. She won. The next morning, the
moment Father opened his eyes, he saw what
Peach had packed for his journey. The ending
is the same as Scenario 1.

3. My father entered the western room
and immediately bolted the door. My sister
was fast asleep. Peach was doing Father's
packing. Obviously she had heard the two
men's conversation and knew that Father was
to set out on the road early the next morning.
Silently Father threw her a glance and saw the
wrinkles on her face and, on the hands with
their thick fingers, scars left by scythes, hemp
ropes, and hard clay clods. As he recalled
how Second Auntie, in her silk finery, never

stopped cracking creamy melon-seeds from
the famous candy store Cai Zhi Zhai and
never ate a meal without some braised pork
in fermented tofu sauce from the celebrated
restaurant Lu Gaojian, an apologetic feeling
washed over him, a feeling that bred tenderness
which, in its turn, lent him strength. With the
same decisiveness that had once driven him
into pulling Peach by the hand and leading her
into the nuptial chamber, he now spread his
arms wide and gathered Peach into his arms.
To his surprise, Peach struggled herself free.
Wondering why she did this, he muttered, "I'll
have to hit the road tomorrow." No sooner
were these words out of his mouth than he
realized that they were quite uncalled for and
even sounded like a plea. With his strong
personality, he felt a surge of indignation now
that he found himself defeated. With thoughts
about male dominance taking full possession
of his mind, he turned Peach around by her
shoulders and, before she could protest,
pushed her onto the bed. In the instant she
fell, Peach felt my eldest brother's kicks in her

belly, which reminded her of what had led to
Father's return and, in particular, of the motives
behind Grandpa's plot. So she tried her hardest
to keep her emotions under control and to let
my father have his way in order to make the
plot successful. However, the weakness, the
yielding, and the reluctant surrender lasted for
only a few seconds before they were replaced by
the physical abhorrence and the psychological
resentment that filled every fiber of her
being. With the strength of a peasant woman
wresting a livelihood from barren soil year in
and year out, she threw my father off her. As
he fell onto the mud floor, caught by surprise,
my sister woke up with a start and began to
wail with abandon. "Grandpa! Grandpa!" she
cried. Each syllable came out loud and clear.

Grandpa in the eastern room heard her. He
had not lain down to sleep. In the darkness
of the night, he had been sitting immobile in
the cold eastern room, running the gamut of
emotions. He dared not intervene when he
heard the hand-to-hand combat, but now that
his granddaughter was crying, he felt entitled

to take the matter into his hands. He went to the main hall and shouted, "Give the girl to me!" The next moment, Father stormed out of the western room, a quilt under his arm, and, without a word, entered the eastern room. Father and son spent the night miserably in one bed. Before dawn, Father started out on the road.

I have no hard evidence to bear out any of these speculations, but I am convinced that one of them was really played out in that clay hut in my ancestral village. Otherwise, in the following year, the news that Peach had given birth to a healthy boy (my eldest brother) wouldn't have given Father such a shock. His eyes grew large with astonishment until they almost popped out of their sockets. Then he gasped with revelation, only to grit his teeth in rage the next moment. He wanted to do something to give vent to his wrath but he kept himself under control and, as the saying goes, chewed bitter herbs and swallowed them in silence. With his quick mind, he had put two and two together and correctly figured out the reason why Grandpa and Peach had teamed up to trick him. From that moment on, he cut off all ties with them.

Two years later, surprisingly enough, Second Auntie conceived and gave birth to my second sister and then, as if there was nothing to stop her, she gave birth to two more daughters, with all three of them one year apart. When my eldest sister was nine years old, Second Auntie did some calculations and concluded that she could do with the help of an unpaid little maidservant and my father, on his part, thought that his aquiline-nosed daughter in his home village was, after all, his own flesh and blood. And so, with husband and wife in agreement, they asked someone who happened to be available to escort the girl from Anhui to Suzhou.

Second Auntie and Father

Before the Japanese attack on Shanghai in 1937, my father's Zhenhua Factory had reached the peak of its glory. The western half of Quanfu Road now belonged to him. With the Wen residence occupying the northern end of the street, his properties stretched almost the whole way south to the Duck Egg Bridge at the crossroads with Stone Street. Anyone reaching cobblestoned Quanfu Road could hear the rumbling of Zhenhua's machines. The rumbling did not come from the aging wool-fluffer. That antiquated machine had long been transferred to a small workshop in Weiting Town dozens of *li* away, to do the

job there for Zhenhua. After raw wool had
been fluffed and cleaned as the first step in the
production process, the resulting fine wool was
transported to Zhenhua to be spun into yarn.
The dust that settled on the floor after the
screening was sold to farmers nearby as a good
fertilizer. Zhenhua Factory had acquired two
more wool-fluffing machines, more than thirty
spinners, and ten carpet-weaving machines—
all electric, human-operated machines. With
the exception of dyeing, which was still
contracted out to a big dye mill in the city
because my father had no confidence in his
dyeing skills, the sequence of operations that
Second Auntie had envisaged years earlier was
by this time basically in place.

Half the credit for the success of the
production line should go to Second Auntie.
Her father's condition had worsened from a
minor stroke to a major one and he eventually
took to his bed, paralyzed. The way things
were in those days, no son would be filial to a
parent long laid up in bed. As another proverb
puts it, when the tree falls, the monkeys

scatter. The mighty Wen family was due for a dramatic decline. However, Miss Wen rose to the occasion. Thanks to her, the power and influence of the Wen family lasted for a few more years. Instead of wishing for her father's death so that she could get her inheritance sooner, Second Auntie, with her unstinting devotion to her father, hired a nurse from the city to take care of him and assigned her loyal servant Mrs. Shen the job of constantly turning Mr. Wen over in bed, rubbing his back, and changing his posture. As a result Old Man Wen remained free of bedsores for years. Second Auntie knew that without bedsores, a paralyzed patient could hang on to life for quite some time. She didn't want her father to die too soon. If he had died, her elder sister and two younger brothers would come to divide up the family fortune. However massive the family fortune might be, how much would she be left with after a four-way division? Her Buddhist mother had passed into nirvana several years earlier, so she was determined to keep her father alive. In the meantime, since she lived in the neighborhood, knew all the contacts, knew how to get things done, and had the necessary experience, she took over the entire Wen family business. Soon thereafter, she sent one of her younger brothers to a college in Shanghai because he had a propensity for learning, and made the other younger brother an accountant at Zhenhua. In no time at all, hers were the only words in the family that counted. She had built for herself quite a reputation for miles around as a filial daughter doing her duty by her father but in fact, she had her father under her thumb and was only using his name to throw her own weight around. She took over every asset that was still under the old man's name. Resolutely she closed the general store and gradually put her father's lifetime of savings into her husband's business. Before long, Zhenhua Factory, that had previously been nothing but a handicraft workshop more dead than alive, underwent renovation and expansion. With new equipment and more workers, Zhenhua began to look like a real factory.

Second Auntie was obsessed by a desire to

outshine others in everything, but she made a poor showing in fertility at first. At the fifteen-table wedding banquet, there was no lack of wishes for early births of sons, but all to no avail. My father attributed her barrenness to her love of Lu Gaojian Restaurant's braised pork in fermented tofu sauce, adding that, just like a hen that did not lay eggs, her excessive body fat clogged up her tubes. There does seem to be some scientific truth to his claim, because one month after Second Auntie lost more than twenty pounds in a bad case of diarrhea, she conceived my second sister. My second sister was born at the very beginning of 1936. At the end of the year, Second Auntie gave birth to my third sister. When the Japanese attacked Shanghai and the bombs flying north almost razed Suzhou's Chang Gate to the ground, she gave birth to my fourth sister. The brick-and-wood factory building with its plentiful stock of wool products was reduced to a pile of rubble in the gunfire. To her credit, Second Auntie, who had just given birth, had the presence of mind to give orders for the three workshops

adjoining the Wen residence to be demolished
before the fire began to spread. With a buffer
zone thus created between the factory and the
residential quarters, the entire family managed
to keep a roof over their heads. However,
Master Wen had such a shock that he suffered
a brain hemorrhage and died before the smoke
thinned out from the rubble where the factory
had stood.

My father almost threw himself on the
tracks of the Shanghai-Nanjing Railroad. He
walked to and fro in front of the smoldering
rubble, with the rumbling of the machines still
echoing in his ears. He thought he could see,
indistinctly, truckloads of wool on their way
into the factory and rolls of wool and carpets
on their way out. But in fact, the workers were,
on their own initiative, clearing away the rubble
in the hope of finding some equipment or
parts that might be used after the resumption
of operations. As Second Auntie dragged him
home, he kept muttering to himself, "I should
have relocated. I should have relocated." Second
Auntie was pained by this. What had happened

was that when the battle of Shanghai was still brewing, owners of wool factories in Shanghai had organized a Relocation Committee. The central government in Nanjing had given the committee its approval. All wool factories, large and small, were urged to relocate to Wuhan, Chongqing, or Kunming. My father had eagerly answered the call, not only because he had enough education to know that assets owned by the Chinese must not be turned over to the conquering enemy, but also because he wanted to keep his business, which had just begun to prosper after he had put in so many years of hard work. But Second Auntie held him back. "Look at my belly," she said. "How far can I go? And look at Baobao who can barely run and Beibei who can barely walk! What are you going to do about them?"

Father countered, "If we really want to go, of course we can do it. Haven't other people moved out? If everything else fails, I'll go to Wuhan on my own first and take the equipment there. After I've set up the factory there I'll come back to get you. What do you say?"

Her eyes bulging, Second Auntie yelled, "If you want to go, go ahead, but don't take the factory with you! The factory doesn't belong to you alone. More than half of it is under the name of Wen! Everyone knows Wuhan is a hot furnace of a place. Suzhou is where I live and Suzhou is where I will die!"

As they argued and fought, the opportunity for relocation slipped by. Soon Second Auntie gave birth to her third daughter. By that time, Shanghai had already been reduced to a river of blood, with corpses floating down Suzhou Creek. It was impossible for Father to go anywhere, much as he wanted to get out.

Second Auntie felt guilty. Believing herself to be, after all, a woman with more hair than wits, she regretted having held her husband back and made the wrong decision at a moment of life-and-death. Seized with fear, she never took so much as a step from my father's side, in case he killed himself while she was not looking. One day, when Father was smiling at his three adorable girls with their aquiline noses, she took advantage of his sunny mood and told him her secret.

"Listen! I have put aside a nice amount of private savings. It may not be enough to start up another Zhenhua with, but if you are willing to settle for less, we can wait until the war is over, and sell half of our land and start a smaller factory. Spinning can still be contracted out, as before. My savings should be enough to cover everything."

With that, she opened a trunk, retrieved a small toilette box filled with gold and silver jewelry and showed it to my father. It contained a sizable diamond ring, the one she had bought with the gifts of money for their wedding. Even though this was by no means enough for them to restore Zhenhua to its pre-war scale, Father still found himself heartened and comforted. His suicidal thoughts receded at last.

10

Grandpa and Auntie Peach

Grandfather, Auntie Peach, my eldest sister and my eldest brother in Anhui almost all perished in the flames of war that same year.

I have no idea whether the commanders of the invading Japanese army, especially the officers directing the battles in Northern Anhui, were aware of Emperor Qianlong's commentary on the region: "Unfruitful hills, unfriendly waters; untamed women, unruly men." I suppose they were. Otherwise, they would not have been so keenly interested in killing and burning after they occupied my ancestral village. Since there was nothing to be looted in that impoverished place anyway,

they thought they might as well burn down
everything. Since the women were untamed
and the men unruly, why not kill them all to
make matters simpler? I have carefully read
the county records and made a good number of
index cards, and I learned that in the first two
years of the War of Resistance against Japanese
Aggression, the Japanese soldiers killed 9,000
civilians of the county where my ancestral
village is. At that time, the entire population of
the county was 30,000. And goodness knows
how many houses were burned down.

By the time the Japanese soldiers charged
into the Xuan Family Village, Grandpa and
Auntie Peach, each carrying a child, had already
fled. Since the Chinese Nationalist army had
withdrawn without putting up a fight, why
should the villagers unnecessarily lay down
their lives for their country? Not a single soul
stayed behind. The Japanese soldiers burned
down the whole village. Instead of leaving
right after they set the village on fire, they
gleefully watched the raging flames spread
from the village to the surrounding areas, from

flat land to the hills, and over the ripened but unharvested wheat fields. It was only after all the crop, the weeds, and the trees of varying heights were scorched and consumed in the fire that the Japanese soldiers began to pull out, satisfied with their work.

Unfortunately, the majority of the villagers were hiding in the surrounding wheat fields and thickets. The crop of that year had been doing unusually well, with the ears big and plump and the stalks dense, tall, and erect. The villagers pressed themselves flat against the ground amid the wheat stalks, earthworm fashion, wishing they could find holes in the ground to crawl into. After the flames began to spread, a good many of the villagers were burned to death. Those who jumped up in an attempt to run from the fire became targets for the Japanese soldiers enjoying the spectacle, giving them some shooting practice. Those lying flat on their stomachs either stayed put and were burned to death or jumped up and got shot. By the time the Japanese departed, more than half of the villagers had perished.

In that life-or-death moment, Grandpa did full justice to his manly spirit and the Xuan family's hereditary high IQ. As he watched the flames sweeping toward the wheat field where all four members of the family were hiding, he suddenly remembered that there was a small pond nearby. Though it had all dried up, at least there was nothing inflammable in it. Without a moment's delay, he told Auntie Peach to carry my big brother in one arm and pull Big Sister with the other, and to move in the direction of the pond, bending as low as possible. He himself took off his shirt, deliberately stood up, and waved his shirt in the air while moving toward the pond from another direction by a roundabout route. Not being particularly tall, he waved his shirt to fool the bullets and, indeed, quite a few of them skimmed over his scalp. When he reckoned that Peach and the children had already arrived at the pond, he made a feint of being hit by a bullet and resolutely threw himself down in the direction of the burning wheat field. No sooner had the firing ceased than he ran at full gallop and leaped into the dried-up pond. As he tumbled onto Peach, he realized that he had been shot in one calf. From then on he walked with a limp.

Even to this day, I still cannot figure out how Grandpa and Peach had managed to get through the eight long years of the war. The Xuan Family Village was reduced to ashes and most of the villagers were displaced and ended up begging just to survive. Many of them died in strange places, putting an end to their family lines. But my grandfather, after leaving the pond, marched the whole family back to what was left of their home and remained there for the rest of his life. During this long period of time, with each day dragging on painfully as if it were a year, they never received even one penny from my father!

Part II

11

Father and Second Auntie

The Japanese bombs had wiped Zhenhua Factory from the face of the earth. In the snap of a finger, my father, proud owner of Zhenhua, was reduced to the humble status of a live-in son-in-law at the mercy of the Wen family's charity. In a matter of days he took up smoking and drinking and had to ask Second Auntie for money to sustain the habits, because he no longer had a penny to his name. He became a man of few words and grew thinner by the day. On his face, with its sharply chiseled features, the erstwhile black eyes had lost all their luster, and the aquiline nose became so prominent that it could very well have served as a peg.

One day he was idly walking down Quanfu Road. At Duck Egg Bridge he ran into a Japanese soldier. According to the rules of those days, Father was supposed to bow and get out of the way. But, staring vacantly in front of him, he kept right on and brushed past the Japanese soldier. The Japanese staggered back and, with a swoosh, drew out his sword. Luckily, an old neighbor of my father's was there by the side of the road. Alarmed at this ominous turn of things, he quickly approached the soldier and, bowing and scraping, his face wreathed in ingratiating smiles, he pointed at my father who had come to a halt and said apologetically, "Sir! This is a mad man. A lunatic! Simply crazy!"

Those were the days when the word "sick," a common euphemism for father's condition, was not to be thrown lightly about. The heavy civilian casualties had brought on a variety of contagious diseases that spread around Suzhou. Calling every sickness a "plague," the Japanese had been making short work of every sick person they laid their eyes on. That neighbor was a smart man.

Second Auntie was afraid that Father would indeed take leave of his senses, but she kept her fears to herself. Apart from consoling Father with assurances about her ample private savings, she resorted to every trick she could think of to keep him at home. She found out that only when my second and third sisters were clinging to him and my fourth sister was chuckling to his face would his dull eyes brighten up with a soft light and a hint of a smile appear on his lips. A more important reason Second Auntie wanted to keep him indoors was that if he found himself on Quanfu Road, he would pace to and fro on the site where the factory had once stood, like a caged wolf in a zoo. Sometimes he would sit on a charred cement post on the site and stare into space for house, even after evening had come. Second Auntie had no alternative but to resort to the carrot-and-stick approach to keep him within the confines of their home, in case he lost his mind as she feared he would. So my father lost not only his factory and his assets but also his freedom. As the saying goes, a clay statue of Buddha crossing a river is hardly able to save itself, let alone others. In my father's condition, he certainly could not afford to concern himself with the well-being of his wife, his father, and the children up north, not to mention the fact that ever since the birth of my eldest brother, he had already revengefully banished from his mind all sense of responsibility toward the old imperial patriarch and his, the emperor's, number-one wife.

My father did not regain his freedom until after Second Auntie's brother-in-law paid a visit to the Wen residence—the very brother-in-law who owed his freedom to Father's trip to the Shanghai Garrison Headquarters. He was still in his old job as a journalist. The newspaper he worked for, located in one of the concessions in Shanghai, not yet under Japanese occupation, was still able to carry articles protesting against the Japanese aggression. The purpose of his trip to Suzhou was to collect data about the losses sustained by Chinese entrepreneurs during the Japanese invasion into the Suzhou and Wuxi region.

After he sat for a while, he pulled Second Auntie into a side room on some pretext, and unceremoniously gave her a piece of his mind. "Do you intend to keep your husband in confinement until he goes raving mad? Is the Wen residence a prisoner-of-war camp run by the Japanese or is it the Shanghai Garrison Headquarters' jail?"

Second Auntie felt grievously wronged. "But I am a good provider to him! I do right by him! And I've already asked someone to go to his home village and bring his eldest daughter to Suzhou! I can't even feed my own three girls and yet, out of the goodness of my heart, I'm sending for that country bumpkin as a favor to him. How have I done anything to hurt him?"

With a snort of contempt, the big-shot journalist from Shanghai replied, "Oh, Second Auntie, spare me your eloquence, please! I can't care less about your motive in getting that girl. You are just the way your sister describes you: You can be super smart about trivialities and do everything to perfection, but in important matters, I'm afraid your short-sightedness will land you in big trouble! Now get this right: Your Xuan Zhigao is no chicken or duck or dog or cat to be raised in a cage. He is someone who left his parents at age fourteen, with his heart set on pushing his fortune in the world and making something of himself. If you really want to be a good dutiful wife, give your private savings to him this minute, so that he can do something to revive his factory! Now I don't mean to scare you, but if you go on keeping him cooped up at home like this for another few months, you can send him either to the madhouse or to the West Hill Funeral Home!"

With that, the journalist who, after all, had been making a living for so many years in the cosmopolitan metropolis of Shanghai, went to talk some sense into Father, leaving Second Auntie in the side room with a vacant look on her face. "Brother!" said the journalist. "Why don't you make a fresh start? Doesn't the factory site still belong to you? Sell off some of it and buy a small workshop! So, there are no more supplies of raw material? Well, I have to say that you have a one-track mind! Why don't you take a look around the concessions of Shanghai? It may look like an isolated island, but in fact it's even more prosperous than before the war! I'm not sure if there's wool to be had in Shanghai, but the fact is, there's any number of restaurants and teahouses from First Avenue to Sixth Avenue, all of them swarming with brokers that deal in all kinds of commodities. Don't hold on to your old way of doing things, replenishing your stock and delivering goods all by yourself. Go out and see the world!"

These words of advice opened a door for my father. The dying embers in his heart burst into flames again. Second Auntie also very wisely accepted her brother-in-law's counsel and, a few days later, released my father from "house arrest" and told her brother who had worked as a Zhenhua accountant to buy a train ticket for my father's journey to Shanghai.

That was in the spring of 1940.

12

My Father and My Mother

The story of how my parents met is romantic and thrilling, but a little clichéd.

That was not Father's first trip to Shanghai. Two years earlier, he had traveled between Suzhou and Shanghai a good many times to find new markets for Zhenhua's products. However, even in its heyday, Zhenhua was no match for any large factory. Because of its limited access to funds and technology, the carpets it turned out were of low or medium grade, but Shanghai was a city with an intriguing pattern of consumption: Upscale and expensive merchandise lavish in appearance but low in practical value sold much faster than cheap and run-of-the-mill but highly functional goods. That was why Zhenhua's products had never been able to find their way into the Shanghai market. Feeling frustrated at last after several futile trips, Father turned his eyes toward medium-and-small-sized cities inland. Shanghai, the land of adventures, intimidated him. But now, that "isolated island" being his only hope, he saw nothing for it but to pull himself together for another try. Like the Liang Mountain rebels depicted in the classic novel *Outlaws of the Marsh*, he was driven to such a move in a moment of desperation.

Now this trip to Shanghai was unlike all his earlier ones. This time, he went there not to sell his products but to find raw material. So instead of doing his rounds of the stores and wholesale departments, as had been his wont, he followed his brother-in-law's advice and zeroed in on the restaurants and teahouses with the largest concentration of brokers. With his experience and business acumen, he quickly caught on. The truth of the matter was that Shanghai, by no means a wool producing

area, had, surprisingly enough, the largest
Wool Exchange in the country. Those with
enough capital had access not only to the high-
grade wool of Xinjiang and Qinghai, but also
Spanish merino wool and Australian wool.
The large textile mills of Shanghai, to which
my father's Zhenhua did not even come close,
did their business in the city and picked up
the raw material directly at the wharf or train
station or even the airport. In contrast, he,
owner of Zhenhua, had to take on everything
himself and go on his travels, whatever the
distance, to check the wool bag by bag in the
wool-producing areas, negotiate the price,
go through the procurement formalities, and
send the shipments to Suzhou. When the bags
were unloaded, he would also get moving and
carry a bag or two on his own shoulder.

Father's eyes were opened. He felt
uncomfortable in the company of brokers who
raked in fat commissions by doing nothing
more than giving their tongues a workout
in teahouses abuzz with conversation and
engaging in speculation without having to put

up a penny. In fact he detested them, and on
the spur of the moment, was not able to make
up his mind on any specific transaction for
which he would have to pay a stiff fee. But at
least he now had a pretty good idea as to how
things stood. It had never occurred to him that
in the wake of a massive war, when so many
Chinese had no home or country to call their
own, there would still be such a blessed place
in the heart of a major metropolis in the east
of China. Confidence and hope came back to
him.

He could not tear himself away from
"Heavenly Bliss" on First Avenue and "Blue
Lotus Pavilion" on Fourth Avenue. He learned
by heart the schedule of the brokers frequenting
these two large teahouses. At Heavenly Bliss,
dealers in wool were most active between the
hours of 10:00 am and 12:00 noon. The rest of
the morning belonged to dealers in hardware.
Dealers in silk and cotton would descend on
the teahouses in droves in the afternoon. After
leaving the session at Heavenly Bliss, he would
go for a bath in Clean Virtue Bathhouse next

to Tianchan Theater, after which he would order some tiny steamed soup buns and take a nap. Then he would join the wool brokers in Blue Lotus Pavilion next to the guesthouse on Fourth Avenue for their two o'clock gathering. Ordering a cup of tea for one copper coin, he would sit there for two or three hours, enjoying the conversation about the price of wool and other information about the market. The war had destroyed ten years of painstaking work, but now, a few days was all it took for the trauma to heal.

His passion for life was rekindled. Upon first arriving in Shanghai, he carelessly put on himself a Chinese long gown belonging to his father-in-law over a wrinkled pair of Western pants. This clash of style drew scornful looks and unkind remarks that mystified him at first, but quickly, light dawned on him: In Shanghai with all its glamour, people were judged not by the worth of their character but snobbishly by the clothes and hats they wore. The very next day, he went to see Second Auntie's sister and borrowed from his brother-in-law a gently used and still quite presentable suit for street wear. His brother-in-law being also big and tall, that dark blue striped suit looked as if it had been tailor-made for my father. Second Auntie's sister, though a housewife, was nevertheless more generous than Second Auntie. With a clap of her hands, she said, "This suit looks so good on you, brother-in-law! You take it!" At the same time, she pressed my father into replacing his cotton shoes with her husband's rubber-soled leather shoes. After knocking about the downtown area for a few days, arrayed in this finery, my father began to pick up urban tastes. One day, at Clean Virtue Bathhouse, he had his disheveled hair cut, blow-dried and parted fashionably on one side of his head. He also acquired the habit of shaving with a Double Arrow razor every morning.

After having learned all there was to know about the wool market in Shanghai's foreign concessions, Father decided to return to Suzhou because he had been counting the days and he believed my eldest sister would soon be arriving in Suzhou. In spite of his callousness to his family in his home village, he still had a soft spot for his little girl. Even though he had spent only one afternoon and one night with her, her round black eyes and her charming little nose stole his heart. He knew full well that she was his child beyond a shadow of a doubt—the eldest princess born to the number-one wife. That brief impression of her convinced Father that this girl would be prettier and smarter than his three daughters by Second Auntie. Afraid that petty, sharp-tongued, and merciless Second Auntie would mistreat her, he eagerly bought a ticket for the first train to Suzhou the next morning.

So he was to leave Shanghai the next morning. As soon as he went through the gate of the Suzhou Train Station the next day, he would have to bow to helmet-wearing Japanese soldiers. The moment he entered the Wen residence, he would have to be prepared to report all his expenses to Second Auntie. With Second Auntie doing the sums in her head and her brother clicking the beads on the abacus, Father would in fact also be giving an account of everything he had done. Depressed by these thoughts, he left Blue Lotus Pavilion but was in no mood to return to his inn at Sha Market on Jiangxi Road. He turned a corner and headed for Tianchan Theater. A small traveling troupe of singers, from goodness knows where, was playing the Anhui opera "Sorrows in the Han Palace." My father had seen the twenty-feet-tall poster some days earlier but had been too busy to see the opera. Now he was determined to give himself a treat that evening.

The melancholy of the opera cast a spell over Father. The familiar melodies and the recitations in his local dialect touched him so deeply that his eyes misted over quite a few times. Overcome with emotion, he told himself that, deep down, he was still a member of the Xuan Family Village in northern Anhui.

As he was exiting the theater after the show was over, he caught whiffs of the aroma of pancakes being grilled with chopped chives and cream. He suddenly became aware of a pang of hunger, the supper he had eaten more than three hours earlier having already dissolved amid his sighs of emotion. Looking into the distance, he saw that the entire Yunnan Road that led to First Avenue in the north and Fifth Avenue down south was thronged with stalls selling food of every variety. Lit by kerosene lamps, acetylene lamps, neon lights, plus burning firewood and coal briquettes, the street was even more a hive of activity than during the daytime. Feeling spasms of hunger in his empty stomach, my father now had first-hand experience of the charms of Shanghai. After all, Shanghai was worlds apart from Suzhou, let alone the Xuan Family village. By the Chang Gate of Suzhou, even on Stone Street, the stores put up their shutters as soon as dusk fell. Only thieves loved to prowl about under cover of night. As for his home village in Anhui, everyone went to bed right after supper, after the chickens had returned to their coops and the birds to their nests.

Now that the differences between urban and rural lives had been brought home to him, my father felt his spirit lifted and decided to go for a late-night snack. He walked south, in the opposite direction to his lodgings. If he went north, he would have to pass Fourth Avenue, and he loathed that street with its crowds of prostitutes. Joy House, a brothel known throughout the city, was right across from Tianchan Theater. My father did not want those unclean women to tug at him and soil the thin woolen suit his brother-in-law had given him. So he headed for Fifth Avenue. He remembered that there were several Muslim noodle restaurants that he liked. The two *mu* of land of the Xuan family grew only wheat and corn, so Father continued to find noodles and steamed buns more appealing than rice.

He ordered a large bowl of noodles tossed in sesame oil and sprinkled with chopped green onions, and ate with relish, feeling like a Shanghainese enjoying the nightlife.

It was almost midnight when he left Fifth Avenue and walked toward his lodgings. With the strong sense of direction of a peasant, he knew his way around. Taking big strides, he kept to the small alleys to find shortcuts, the cobblestoned surface of the alleys echoing with the clicks of the nails on the heels of his leather shoes.

Even though this was a bustling part of town, the small alleys were quiet by this time of the night. After crossing Fourth Avenue and Third Avenue, Father was approaching Sha Market on Second Avenue when he heard a clatter of footsteps, followed immediately by a woman's stifled scream. It was all too obvious that a woman was being assaulted. Father stopped in his tracks and looked intently in the direction of the mouth of the lane where the noise had come from. He saw two men, each holding a shiny object, pushing a tall, thin, and delicately constituted young man against the wall. The youngster was busily searching in his own pockets, moving one hand down the other arm, and handing whatever he took off to the two men. From the depths of the alley came another stifled, blood-curdling scream. It was the same woman's voice. Father moved a few steps forward. Now he was conducting himself like a northern Anhui native ignorant of the ways of Shanghai. A Shanghainese would

never do the same under such circumstances.
Imagine drawing closer to a crime when any
other man would not be able to take to his
heels quickly enough!   The criminal gangs
of Shanghai robbed, killed, and kidnapped
people every day.   In the last few years, there
had been a proliferation of undercover agents
of the Nationalist Party, the collaborationist
government, and the Communist Party. The
Japanese dominated the Chinese sections of
the city and the British and Americans and
the French held sway in the concessions. The
Chinese having been reduced to the lowest
class in their own city, what was the point of
meddling in other people's affairs and inviting
trouble? Therefore, even though the screams
for help were audible throughout the alley,
no window lit up; no one stepped out to help,
much less a Buddha or a hero out of the blue to
deliver the victims from distress.

As if by predestination, Father happened
to be at the mouth of that alley at that
moment. Although he had learned to enjoy
"nightlife," he had not yet trained himself to

be a true Shanghainese. Having inherited my grandmother's robust constitution, aquiline nose, and strong character, and having just fortified himself with a bowl of noodles tossed in sesame oil and sprinkled with chopped green onions, my father roared at the two thugs and the victim, "What do you think you are doing?"

Father was a baritone with a nice acoustic resonance in his broad chest. Tall and powerfully built, he looked even more imposing in his fine suit, and he spoke with a northern Anhui accent. (His accent stayed with him into his old age. As for the Suzhou and Shanghai dialects, he only managed to be able to understand them but never learned to speak them.) To the ears of the Shanghainese, the northern Anhui dialect was indistinguishable from Mandarin. Very few Shanghainese could make out the differences among the dialects of Anhui, Shandong, Henan, Hebei, or even between Shaanxi and Shanxi. Upon hearing my father's mighty shout, the two thugs mistook him for a soldier or an officer of one of the rival factions. Moreover, under the dim streetlamp, my father's overall image was menacing enough to deter them. What set Shanghai gangsters apart from other people was the fact that they bullied the weak and cringed before the strong. After a two-second hesitation, the two thugs shouted something in their own code at their accomplice further down the alley, abandoning their victim—a tall and thin young man. In a flash, they disappeared without a trace.

Father had not expected such an easy victory. Feeling doubly confident now as a champion of justice, he made a dart toward the youngster still in a daze, meaning to help him take on the remaining thug and rescue the other victim, who was obviously his female companion. To my father's surprise, the young man jumped aside as if shocked by electricity and, without a second thought, showed a clean pair of heels. With a speed faster than that of the two thugs, he vanished from view. My father spat indignantly in the direction he had gone, turned around, and stormed into the alley with even greater resolve.

It was a narrow alley. Father, coming in from the outside, had no way of concealing his entrance. The thug, who had already had plenty of warning, hid in the shadows. With one sweeping movement of his leg, he brought my father to the ground. My father scrambled to his feet but before he had recovered his balance, he received a heavy blow right in the face. He almost fell into the trash can near the entrance of the alley. Father had never done justice to his big frame by learning martial arts or qigong. He was a businessman, interested in opening factories, not in brawling. He didn't take physical assaults well. His head in a swirl, he collapsed against the dirty cement wall near the trash can, thus clearing the way for that kung fu master to pass through the narrow alley. Though the thug had scored a few points with the movements of his fist and foot, he wasn't going to stick around just for the fun of fighting. Now that he had a clear escape route, why not make good use of it and get out of there? With one movement of his body, he was gone, leaving my father behind, leaning against the wall and wiping blood from his nose in a none-too-dignified posture.

Inside the alley, a girl was cowered in a heap. Her blouse had been torn but she was otherwise unhurt. Nineteen years of age at the time, she was later to be my mother.

13

My Oldest Sister and Second Auntie

My father and Second Auntie asked someone to escort my eldest sister to Suzhou. In fact, Father had been planning to have the man work for him once Zhenhua was resurrected. When it comes to seniority in the Xuan clan, I should call him grand uncle because he was my father's uncle once removed. My grand uncle was half deaf and half mute. No one wanted to marry him. So his branch of the clan came to an end with him. Even though he was hard of hearing and couldn't make himself understood clearly, he was extremely clever with his hands, especially in carpentry. One look at an article made of wood was enough for him to reproduce it, accurate to the last detail. In fact he could make the replica even more exquisite and of greater practical value. Once when he was working for a rich man in the county, he had followed his employer to the Suzhou region on a trip and stayed for a few days in a side room in the Wen residence. In the beginning, Second Auntie turned up her nose at that dirty and stupid-looking country bumpkin and agreed to let him stay for only one night. To her surprise, before the night was out, he had fixed every broken basin and bucket and even a tottering bed abandoned in that side room. Second Auntie's face brightened. Effusively she insisted that he stay longer. As it turned out, my grand uncle fixed all the wooden pieces of furniture in the house and, as a bonus, gave new life to the dozen or so beat-up spinning wheels belonging to Zhenhua. After my grand uncle returned to Anhui, Second Auntie often thought of him, but each time not before something had been broken. My father was not that utilitarian, but he made a mental note of the man's skills. And so, when he was planning to resurrect Zhenhua from its own ashes, he naturally called this relative to mind. As coincidence would have it, my grand uncle wrote him a letter, offering his services if needed, because life in the village was too hard. The timing could not have been better. My grand uncle had taught himself to read and had written that letter himself. My father wrote him a reply, asking him to take my eldest sister with him. My father's letter said, "Please relay this message for me: In these hard times, let me support the girl. I will not write a separate letter." The reason Father chose not to "write a separate letter" was known only to my grandfather and Auntie Peach. But in the Xuan Family Village, as was to be expected, the villagers burst into heated condemnation of my father.

One said, "So, as soon as she's old enough to carry wild herbs and cut grass, he whisks her away. Peach is one luckless woman!"

Another villager said, "It's obvious that the girl is going to work as a maid."

"Poor thing!" There was a chorus of agreement.

But to my grandfather and Peach they offered these comforting words: "Your girl's life is finally going to change for the better. She'll be a young lady of the city!"

"For better or for worse, she's going to join her own father. She won't be hard done by!"

"You can relax!" Everybody sang the same tune.

They were not saying one thing and meaning another. They just did not have the heart to speak their minds when my grandfather and Peach were already overtaken by grief, as if this was a matter of life and death.

Father had not yet returned from Shanghai when my eldest sister arrived in Suzhou. It was supper time. To her credit, Second Auntie was not oblivious to proper etiquette. She told Mrs. Shen the servant to add two pairs of chopsticks for Grand Uncle and Big Sister. Mrs. Shen had been with the Wens for so many years that she was almost a member of the family. When the kindhearted Mrs. Shen filled the rice bowls, she tamped each filling down and added more until two peaks formed. Resenting Mrs. Shen's generosity, Second Auntie gave her a dark look.

Big Sister wolfed the rice down until she almost choked. Ignoring the dishes and the soup, she just kept raking the rice into her mouth. Second Auntie spoke up in her sing-song intonation, "What's the big rush? You'll have enough food to eat every day. You're not out on the street begging for leftovers or charity gruel."

Big Sister, having just left Anhui, did not understand a word of Second Auntie's Suzhou dialect, which can hide thorns in its soft tones. However, she caught on to something from the way Second Auntie screwed down the corners of her mouth and tossed her head. The little girl fixed her black eyes on Second Auntie for several seconds until Second Auntie broke off. Second Auntie said later to Father, "Her eyes are exactly like yours. When she looks at me, I get a feeling that it's you looking at me!"

No sooner had Second Auntie broken off than Big Sister laid down her chopsticks. Mrs. Shen off to one side said eagerly, "Eat some

more! There's more in the pot!" But my sister
remained motionless. Second Auntie flared
up. "Good gracious!" said she. "You haven't
even washed off the mud all over you and
you are already acting high and mighty, my
Number-One Young Mistress! What did I say
to deserve this tantrum?"

With hindsight, I believe this outburst of
Second Auntie's was the height of stupidity.
Big Sister, having just come from the north,
did not even know the pronouns in the Suzhou
dialect. Why would she throw a tantrum over
something Second Auntie said? She was only
nine years old. Would she even dare? In actual
fact, it was Second Auntie herself who raised my
sister's place in the family. As a concubine, she
was tormented by a sense of inferiority deep in
her psyche. She may have put on a brave face,
but deep down, she felt insecure. She knew
all too well that as long as Peach was alive, she
could not be made Number-One. She was also
stupid in being the first one to call Big Sister
"Number-One Young Mistress." Henceforth
Big Sister was officially known as "Number-

One Young Mistress," and Second Auntie's three daughters were demoted to "Number-Two," "Number-Three," and "Number-Four" young mistresses.

The object of Second Auntie's outburst, my eldest sister, without knowing the first thing about what Second Auntie was saying in her soft, sing-song intonation, kept her eyes fixed on Second Auntie. She did not feel wronged. Actually, all that talk meant nothing to her. While Second Auntie was trying to regain her composure, Big Sister spoke up, "Keep the food for my mother."

Her voice was crisp, her enunciation clear, her accent exactly the same as my father's. In her filial devotion to her mother, she, in a neither too-servile nor too-overbearing manner, announced to Second Auntie's face her loyalty to her own mother. Second Auntie almost choked from sheer rage. She flung down her rice bowl and flew into her own room. The next day, when my father returned from Shanghai, he found her eyes still slightly red and swollen.

14

My Mother and My Father

My father was back in Suzhou in body, but he had left his heart in Shanghai.

My mother's oval face with its spotless fair complexion and her limpid eyes kept appearing before him. Mother was no ravishing beauty but her skin was delicate with a natural, soft luster. Her unpowdered and unrouged cheeks looked a little pale but were as smooth as porcelain and jade. Her eyes were large and sparkling, with the bright whites of her eyes setting off her black pupils to pleasing effect. Her two rows of long and dense dark lashes added to her unsophisticated, demure, soulful, and understated girlish charms. She was tall

and looked so frail that a gust of wind seemed
enough to blow her away. Probably because she
had been born and raised in a major metropolis
and given an enlightened education, she did
not acquire the bad postures that other tall
girls often succumbed to. Her tall and straight
figure lent her a dignified and graceful air. She
was a Shanghai girl of an entirely different
order from Auntie Peach of Anhui and Second
Auntie of Suzhou. Able to tell the differences
among them, my father fell in love with her at
first sight and would never be able to banish
her from his mind. Of course, a thirty-year-
old man and a father of four daughters was
not going to lose his senses altogether. After
returning to Suzhou, he calmly and orderly
set about preparing for the restart of his
factory and, in a strictly businesslike manner,
reported to Second Auntie and her brother on
the conditions of the wool market in Shanghai
and analyzed future prospects—all done
with a feeling that a part of him was lost, as
if he had been split in two. His outer self was
mechanically doing what should be done while

his inner self, if he had a moment to spare, would recall that oval face with its black eyes and fair complexion. The events of that night, along with their conversation, would play out like a movie over and over again in my father's mind, never boring him.

My mother had told my father the story of her life. It was very simple: My grandparents were both primary school teachers. My mother was their only child. My grandparents had been wiped out, along with their school in Zhabei District of Shanghai, in an intense Japanese bombing raid during the War of Shanghai. My mother had just passed the entrance examination for nursing school. She survived but was left all alone. Before she graduated, she found employment in Renji Hospital and had been working as a nurse when she met my father. The tall and thin young man who had deserted her and run for dear life was the son of the fabric store next to the hospital. He had been courting my mother, hoping to make her his wife. Whenever Mother was not on night duty, he would send over tickets to movies and shows and, after the shows were over, would take her on a stroll down the streets, reluctant to let her go. That evening, my mother had been very tired and so, after watching the fourth show of the day at a movie house, she insisted on returning to her nurses' dormitory. But the young dandy, having slept his fill during the day, became a god on night patrol, so to speak, and literally dragged her to the Bund to take in the northwesterly wind. He did not escort my mother back to her dorm until night was quite advanced. They were set upon when they had just reached the cemetery for foreigners, at the corner of Second Avenue and Shandong Road.

As if guided by Providence, my father played the role of a hero rescuing a damsel in distress in kung fu movie. Although he got hit, his nose bled, and his borrowed suit was stained and crumpled, he was, in my mother's eyes, her savior. Though he cut a sorry figure, he felt a surge of manly pride when he realized that the girl squatting on the ground was cutting an even sorrier figure. He decided to put the finishing touch to his heroic deed. In a few strides, he was by my mother's side.

"It's all right now. I'll walk you home."

Still cowered in a heap, my mother refused to budge.

It dawned on my twice-married father that this girl, with her shoulder showing through the tear in her blouse, could hardly be expected to go out on brightly lit Shanghai streets. With one swift movement, Father divested himself of that thin woolen jacket.

"Take this. You'll be OK."

With the jacket draped over my mother's slender frame like a Daoist robe, Mother was reduced to an oval face inlaid with two large eyes.

Even when draped in such a large and thick Daoist robe, she still kept shivering. My father, wearing only a shirt, had to put his arm around her frail shoulders and help her along, as if carrying a sheaf of wheat stalks under his arm.

When they were drawing near Renji Hospital, Mother came to a halt.

"Anything wrong?" Father tried his best to speak softly. "Didn't you say …"

"I can't go back. There are too many people in the dorm. If I'm seen like this, they will talk."

"That's no problem," said Father without missing a beat. "You go to my lodgings. I rented a single room."

My mother raised her head and, for the first time, looked my father in the eye. In that instant, Father was smitten and he fell in love, but, keeping proper control of himself, he met her gaze and said with a tranquil conscience, "I'll go to Clean Virtue Bathhouse. I'm leaving tomorrow morning anyway. I don't live here. The innkeeper is a very nice woman. You can ask her to help you if there's anything you need. I've already paid the bill. Don't worry."

These words revealed another side of him to my mother. If the way he intervened at the entrance of the alley showed his courage and determination to fight for a just cause whenever and wherever he saw one, these thoughtful explanations and arrangements sufficed to exhibit his competence, his considerateness, and his ability to read other people's feelings. My mother felt that Heaven had at last sent her in her forlornness someone she could lean on, someone who was perfect in every way.

Alas, just as no gold is 100% pure, so no man is perfect and flawless. My mother soon learned that my father had a wife in Anhui and another one in Suzhou.

My father never tried to hide anything from my mother. The two of them had a predestined bond. In the presence of Mother, who was a full ten years younger than him, Father just had the urge to say whatever was on his mind. True lovers do not stand guard over each other. Ever since I can remember, I had the feeling that my parents would never run out of conversation. I remember that in our old home in the western part of Shanghai, my parents slept in the inner room and my younger brother and I occupied the outer one. As soon as Father returned home, he would have no end of things to tell Mother. I always drifted off to sleep with Father's buzzing baritone and Mother's soft responses in my ears. The moment I opened my eyes the next morning, I would hear the hum of conversation again in the inner room, as if they had not stopped chatting the whole night. Later, out of curiosity, I strained my ears to make out what they were saying. To my surprise, most of the talk was about wool, yarn, replenishing the stock, and expanding sales, etc. I know that my mother has never understood the wool business. I am mystified as to how she never got bored. Of course, what I know about the history of the Xuan family actually came, in the large part, from my eavesdropping on their private conversations.

I cannot stifle my urge to suspend my account of the family history and launch into some comments on the love between a man and a woman. I think there is nothing more wonderful, complex, unreasonable, and illogical than love. There is no pattern to be found, no rights and wrongs to judge. No explanation of love can cover it, because love knows no bounds. No one single definition can apply to it. To avoid sounding fanciful, let me do a concrete analysis of my parents' case. Isn't it often said that love is based on shared hobbies and interests? Well, my father is every inch a businessman, with a keen interest in economic affairs, but my mother doesn't know the first thing about money matters. When she was poor, she felt no urge to get rich. When she was rich, she did not get above herself. All her life, she never cared much about money. Isn't it often said that the husband sings and the wife follows, and that only when the wife helps the husband in his career would the two make a perfect like-minded couple? According to this logic, Second Auntie should be the perfect partner for my father and the two should benefit from each other's company. As it turned out, Father regularly hid things from her and never told her the top secret of the Xuan family, my eldest brother's lineage, not even when she was on her deathbed. But Second Auntie was no fool. Over the long years of their married life, she sensed something out of the ordinary about my father's iciness towards his first son. Once, when talking about Father's home village, and happening to be in a fury, she blurted out, "That bastard!" My father's eyes bulged and he almost gave her a slap across the face, thus effectively putting an end to her suspicions. But to my mother, my father willingly laid bare everything voluntarily. Without mincing words, he unburdened himself of that unspeakable secret to her, only a nineteen-year-old girl at the time.

"That boy is my father's son. In our dialect, that's called 'raking in the ashes,' meaning incest. If others get to know about this, even our ancestors eight generations back would suffer from the disgrace!"

As if she were listening to the *Thousand and One Nights*, Mother's jaw dropped. It was some time before she commented with a sigh, "So pitiful!"

"Who is pitiful?" My father was bewildered.

"Everyone involved is," replied Mother, with tears welling up in her eyes.

When talking about Second Auntie, Mother always said longingly, "She is so capable. You

owe so much to her. I wish I were more like
her, so that I wouldn't always get browbeaten,
and I could give you a hand."

They began to have such intimate
conversations about a month after they first
met. Mother had already moved out of the
dorm to a second-floor room in the back
wing of the small inn at Sha Market. The
innkeeper, having taken a deposit from my
father, rented the room to my mother on a
long-term basis. Because the deposit was quite
substantial, the monthly rent was reduced to a
nominal minimum. My mother had no head
for money matters so she was completely in
the dark, and the innkeeper, following my
father's instructions, kept her mouth shut.
So for quite a long time, Mother thought
that she had chanced upon a good deal and a
good innkeeper not preoccupied with making
money. Believing she did not owe anyone any
favors, she proudly moved out of her dorm.
This event alone goes to show that my father
was not so much older than my mother for
nothing. This twice-married man knew how

to help the woman he loved without giving himself away, managing to avoid hurting her pride.

My mother had to move. After making a poor showing that night, the young dandy of the fabric store went to see her again in all brazenness the very next day, but my mother acted as if she did not know him. She took no notice of him, but she did not mock him, either. She just kept her eyes down and gave him to understand that she was not going to be his woman. The young dandy was incensed. Shanghai dandies might not know how to deal with thugs but when it came to a little nurse, they could out-thug the thugs. He began to spread vicious rumors among my mother's acquaintances, saying that he knew my mother was no longer a virgin and therefore he had long decided to jilt her. In a pre-emptive strike, he invented another falsehood, saying that the man who waylaid my mother that night was a former lover of hers, and that the big, dark, and fat northerner was an undercover police agent, thus piecing unrelated elements together into a graphic story. As a result, tongues wagged behind my mother's back whenever she went in and out of the dorm. All alone, my mother had nowhere to hide and nobody she could pour out her tale of woe to. A few days later, Father went back to Shanghai from Suzhou on a business trip, carrying in his bosom a wad of money that Second Auntie had finally approved for him to buy wool with. After getting off the train, Father stopped by Renji Hospital before heading for Blue Lotus Pavilion and asked the custodian to announce him to my mother. Father's northern accent and his vigorous build convinced the old man of the truth of the young dandy's account. He was loath to run errands for that little nurse, but suddenly remembering that this big fellow was an undercover police agent whom it would not be wise to offend, he rushed upstairs to the third floor and called my mother from the delivery room. When my red-faced mother was talking with Father outside, heads wearing wonton-shaped hats popped out of the windows of the second and third floors, and all charges against my mother were confirmed.

Father paid the deposit for Mother without a second thought. It was a substantial amount of money but he already had everything worked out, thanks to his business with the brokers. One had to pay a commission to a broker for an order of raw material, but there were no set rules as to the amounts. Father had seen an opening. He could take a carelessly daubed receipt from one of the brokers, tamper with the figure, and present it to Second Auntie for reimbursement. The worst that could happen was that Second Auntie would curse the broker for his greed, but there was nothing she could do about it. Later, Father didn't even have to go to the trouble of altering the figures. The brokers had known him for years and knew that Father was supporting a family in Shanghai. So when drawing up receipts for their commissions, they were only too happy to take the credit for being helpful. More often than not, they would take the initiative and ask my father, "Boss Xuan, just say the word! How much do you want me to write?"

And then Father's tricks grew larger in scale. He left no loopholes in Zhenhua's account books but, at the same time, he was able to fill his own pockets. He was a businessman, after all, and he had a need for private savings. All inventions start from need.

Sha Market Street with its tumbledown houses crossed First Avenue. In the shadows of the imposing walls, these houses were not much better than the ghettos. The house where Mother rented a room was built of wooden planks. With western exposure, her small room, about a dozen square meters, was bright with sunlight from ten o'clock in the morning to five or six in the afternoon throughout the summer. My parents spent six months in that sweltering room, ardently in love.

With the excuse of rebuilding Zhenhua, Father traveled back and forth between Shanghai and Suzhou. In those six months, he spent much more time in Shanghai than in Suzhou. After he rented that west-facing room for my mother, he booked for himself a bunk bed in Clean Virtue Bathhouse on a long-term basis and was charged per night only the price of one bath ticket. His frugality pleased but also pained Second Auntie. When Father went to claim reimbursement from her, she said apologetically, "You'd better go back to the inn. That room at Sha Market that you used to rent is not that expensive."

Father replied craftily, "The rent went up long ago. And I would have to pay a deposit, too. Would you be willing to do that?"

That reduced Second Auntie to silence.

During his stays in Shanghai, Father left the bathhouse bright and early every morning, went to Blue Lotus Pavilion for a dim sum breakfast, and chatted with regular patrons there over a cup of tea and a dish of dim sum. At eight o'clock, he would go to the entrance of Renji Hospital to meet my mother. In order to fit in with his schedule, Mother had asked to be put on the very unpopular night shift on a regular basis. At the stroke of eight, Mother would take off her wonton-shaped hat, change into casual clothes, and gracefully walk out the gate. My father, well spruced up in his

immaculate suit and shiny leather shoes, would
go toward her from the other side of Shandong
Road and, with the ease born of long practice,
offer her his arm, bent in the shape of the letter
L. Through this strong arm, Mother seemed
to transmit all her overnight fatigue to him,
her tall and frail figure looking like a soft vine
attached to a large cypress tree. Arm in arm,
they went to the plank house where Mother's
room was soon to be flooded with sunlight,
with many eyes fixed on their backs from the
windows and entrance of the hospital. Some
of these looks were envious, some jealous,
some approving, and some contemptuous.
Many people had already learned that my
father was not a policeman but a businessman,
owner of a none-too-big factory that was not
in Shanghai but not far away. Some said that
even though he did not look old, he was about
ten years older than the girl, and that the man
was a northerner, but looked decent enough.
In short, gossip was rife. But no one knew that
my father was a married man. On this point,
my parents kept their lips sealed. However

open-minded, Westernized, and accustomed people were to the multitudes of similar cases, contempt for concubines was not something that could be easily done away with. My parents knew all too well what kind of humiliation leakage of such information would bring to my mother, who remained a virgin at the time. They made every effort to build defensive walls around themselves.

Once in the west-facing room, they let down their guard and breathed easy again. Father would talk endlessly about what he had done in Suzhou in the last few days, how Second Auntie had told him to return to the inn, how he had replied, and what he had heard at breakfast that morning. Mother would brew tea, make coffee, and light a cigarette for Father, and, during the intervals, would nestle quietly in Father's bosom and listen to his melodious northern Anhui dialect. She liked caressing his whiskers with her soft hand, press his aquiline nose with her pointed index finger, and sometimes press her small head against his broad and solid chest to listen

to the resonance inside. Two hours would
quickly fly by. Then my father would check his
watch, jump up, and say, "Oh no! Old Wang
and Pockmark Qian of Heavenly Bliss must
be waiting for me!" Mother would say with a
smile, "I knew the time was already past. I just
didn't want to push you out." Father would
give her a stroke on the cheek by way of saying
goodbye, throw open the door, and be on his
way. Mother would bend over the window
sill and wait for him to emerge from the door
downstairs, watching him until he disappeared
from view. She would then withdraw from the
window and go to bed for a few hours sleep.

After three o'clock in the afternoon, my
father would hasten back to her. Sometimes
they continued their chat in each other's
embrace and sometimes went out, hand in
hand, to stroll around the City God Temple,
watch an afternoon movie show, or do
window-shopping at Xianshi Department
Store or Yong'an Department Store, just like
newlyweds. But after evening set in and
they finished eating supper together, Mother

had to go to the hospital for her night shift. Father would walk her to the entrance before returning to Clean Virtue Bathhouse to retire for the night. He never stayed in Mother's small room overnight.

Both of them took their love seriously. It was, to them, solemn and even sacred. Other people would probably find this unusual. Even I, a product of their love, went to great lengths to do some investigation and research before finally concluding that Father, a northerner with two wives and four daughters, had held nothing more than a platonic relationship with a young and pretty Shanghai girl full of tender feelings, even when they were behind closed doors, wearing scanty summer cloths. He had never made any improper moves.

Actually, it is all very simple if the case is analyzed correctly. Father's marriage to Auntie Peach had been arranged single-handedly by my grandmother. He had been given absolutely no say in the matter. His marriage to Second Auntie was mostly out of utilitarian motives. My mother was his first love. For the first time he experienced spontaneous feelings for someone, while in full control of his actions. He cherished these genuine feelings but, at the same time, he was profoundly aware of his twice-married status, which he would not be able to free himself of any time soon. He knew how cruel such a state of affairs was to my mother, who was as pure as untainted ice and jade. He was in a dilemma. He would never leave her, but not leaving her meant doing her harm, and harming his true love—an innocent girl who loved him back—was the last thing he wanted. Yet he was at a loss as to how he extricates himself. He could do no more than engage in self-deception. He did his best to respect her and cherish her, to make her appreciative of his sincerity, and to perfect his own image as a way of compensating her. As for Mother, she was at an age when she felt the first flowering of love without knowing much of the ways of the world. Her bookish parents had nurtured this purity of mind in their only child and her overly simple experience made her a stranger to the perils of life. Her parents, belonging to the lower stratum of the Shanghai intelligentsia, had been half traditional and half westernized, and were neither poor nor rich. They had brought her up within the confines of their home. However corrupt the culture of glamorous Shanghai was, whatever my mother learned had been filtered, masticated, and ruminated over by her parents-cum-teachers. They took great pains with her education, hoping she would stay unsullied amid a contaminated environment, but in fact, they did her a disservice. In her kindness and weakness, which were dominant traits in her character, she attached herself unhesitatingly, like a vine, to my father when she thought she had met someone who could give her protection and backing. In the beginning, Father's married status had disappointed her and shaken her resolve, but, as time wore on, she gradually came to dismiss its importance. Father's frankness with her convinced her of his trustworthiness. Father's rigorous self-control in their six-month-long relationship won her respect and her faith in him. Within those six

months, both of them were intoxicated by the
sacrosanct and unblemished atmosphere that
they had created for themselves. Therefore,
even when alone in their own Garden of Eden,
no evil snake had enough magic power to
corrupt them, especially my father, who was
already laden with guilt.

Father did everything he could, with zeal
and proper ceremony, to make preparations
for the wedding with my mother, making
it look as if it was his first wedding. He had
just had a windfall, one that Second Auntie
in Suzhou would never be able to find out
about. He had resold a shipment of goods
ordered from Heavenly Bliss to a man from
Qingdao, Shandong, whom he had met at
Blue Lotus Pavilion. The man from Shandong
was in Shanghai on an urgent mission to find
raw material for his factory. So Father played
broker for once. From the resell, he not only
made a profit from the price difference but also
took a commission from the Shandong man, as
was customary. The two sums of money added
up to quite a sizable amount. He lost no time

in booking a two-room apartment—with one large room and one smaller room, one facing south and the other facing north—located on Jinlong Street, a quiet alley connecting Shandong Road with Henan Road south of Fifth Avenue. And he had a carpenter make a complete set of furniture. When September came around, he also had a legal procedure taken care of. He took his half deaf and half mute uncle to a law office in the French Concession and officially declared himself his uncle's adopted son, the purpose of which was to apply with my mother for a formal marriage license. According to the rules prevalent at the time, a marriage license should bear the seal of an approving elder in the clan. So my father made himself his uncle's adopted son and had a seal made for his uncle, which he then affixed to his marriage license, to show that an elder of the clan had approved the marriage. In theory, my mother had become my grand uncle's daughter-in-law. Put another way, if my grand uncle had only one son, my father, and as his son had only one wife, my mother, then it follows that my mother was the number-one wife. It was a very impressive effort that my father made, devising such a time-consuming, expensive, and brain-teasing plan of self-deception and actually putting it into proper execution. The only appreciative and grateful person who used it to comfort and sedate her injured heart was my mother.

The wedding ceremony was held with all due pomp and circumstance in the Guesthouse Restaurant on Fourth Avenue. Even though it was only a ten-minute walk from Sha Market to the Guesthouse Restaurant and then to the new apartment on Jinlong Street, Father still rented a Xiangsheng limousine with golden, silver, red, and green festoons all over it and red paper cuttings of the character for "Double Happiness" posted on the windows, giving my mother a radiant glow of pride in front of her invited colleagues.

During that time, Father's heart had neatly split into two halves: one for Zhenhua and one for my mother. The halves beat as one, leaving no room for other people or other things. To

Second Auntie, he feigned compliance, using a whole repertoire of tricks. As for Auntie Peach, he had ten thousand reasons not to pay her the least attention. Without the slightest qualm, he set up another household in Shanghai. My mother became his "Number-Three Consort."

15

My Mother and Second Auntie

I was born in 1941. Two years later, I had a brother. My mother lost her job soon after she got married. In her delicate health, she showed signs of a possible miscarriage after conceiving me and had to lie in bed all day long. I was born a sick baby and suffered from recurrent bouts of illnesses, major and minor. Mother had to nurse me twenty-four hours a day, and my brother followed closely on my heels. So Mother quit her job and became a housewife.

Those were trying years for Father. His factory had been renamed "Zhenxin Wool Mill." "Xin" [new] replaced "hua" [China] because Shanghai had fallen into Japanese hands. "Wool Mill" replaced "Carpet Factory" because he had deliberately reduced the scale of production. In his frequent trips to Shanghai, he got inspiration from Shanghai's mode of large-scale production. He understood that with his limited means and in the current circumstances, he would be courting failure if he tried to resume his ambitious pre-war production line, to market his factory's own products. Any link in the sequence could go wrong and deal the fragile production line a fatal blow. He must not be blind to reality. He also saw that in China, the time for him to expand his business had not yet arrived. Even survival would be by no means easy. Being a small-time capitalist born to a humble background, he'd better not set his sights too high. Humbly he swallowed his ambition and made the painful decision to reduce the scale of production. The newly started "Zhenxin Wool Mill" had only two workshops—one to fluff wool, the other to spin yarn. In fact, they only processed raw material, becoming one link in a much wider production process.

Those were trying times for Father also because he had to devote all his ingenuity and talent to supporting the three of us, mother and sons, and, at the same time, trying to keep his second family unaware of our existence. My mother and, later, my brother and I with our aquiline noses, brought him happiness and satisfaction but also stress. We were in fact a burden to him. The three of us became the five-finger mountain that sat on the Monkey King's back. The Pacific War broke out in the year I was born. The Japanese seized the foreign concessions, bringing an end to Shanghai's status as an "isolated island." Having turned from a colonized people to a vanquished people, the residents found life even harder than before. It was quite an effort for a small-time businessman like my father to support the three of us. Worse still, the money came out of his private savings. He also had to be constantly on guard against any communication over a hundred-*li* distance between his two homes. Second Auntie, in her petty ways, was already making things difficult for my eldest sister whom my father had virtually abandoned. If she got to know that there was a young woman in Shanghai, raising a family with my father, the consequences would be unthinkable. Well aware of what a holy terror Master Wen's daughter was, my father strove to build a dyke to protect his secret and spent every day in those four to five years on edge.

The dyke finally burst.

The problem was with a young and rash wool broker. He didn't do it on purpose. He just wanted to transfer to my father some remnant stocks of a factory going out of business and went to Heavenly Bliss and Blue Lotus Pavilion on two consecutive days to look for my father. Father was busy transporting that beat-up wool-fluffing machine from Weiting back to Suzhou. The tiny workshop in Weiting had folded and the machine was sitting there, doing nothing. Father found it still usable, so he bought it back at scrap iron rate. That young broker, not knowing my mother's address on Jinlong Street nor what the veteran brokers knew about the ins and outs of my family's history, went thought-

lessly all by himself to Suzhou, found his way to
Zhenxin Wool Mill on Quanfu Road, and asked
for Mr. Xuan. In Mr. Xuan's absence, the person
in charge—Second Auntie's brother—received
him. Not knowing much about the ways of the
world, the young man had no idea what could
be said and what not. When talking about business matters, he mentioned "Mrs. Xuan" and
"their two sons." Second Auntie, of course, had
only daughters. Being a shrewd man, Second
Auntie's brother asked a few more questions
without betraying his emotion and gained a
pretty good idea of what was going on. Who
would turn against one's own flesh and blood to
help an outsider? Before the young broker had
even walked out of the Chang Gate, the mistress
of the Wen residence had already been tipped
off by her brother.

Second Auntie was having lunch. She
smashed some plates and bowls on the spot,
and gave Big Sister a few slaps across the face
on one pretext or another. After this outburst,
she started thinking and put two and two
together. Father had claimed that trip was to

Weiting, but his prolonged absence could mean only one thing: he must have gone straight to Shanghai from Weiting. The young broker had come to Suzhou only because he had no clue as to the location of that scoundrel Xuan Zhigao's Shanghai love nest! At this thought, she fumed with rage. How she wished she could rip my parents to pieces with her own hands and set them on fire! With her decisiveness and fiery temper, this woman of action brushed aside protests from her confidante, Mrs. Shen, and her brother, who regretted having shot his mouth off now that things appeared to be taking an ugly turn. Without losing a single moment, Second Auntie issued the following order to all occupants of the Wen residence: "Lock up the gate behind us! Everyone is to follow me to Shanghai!"

It was a mighty expeditionary army consisting of four girls and four adults, Mrs. Shen, Second Auntie's brother and Big Sister among them. After having been slapped across the face twice for no good reason and then told abruptly not to go to school but follow everyone

else to Shanghai, my fourteen-year-old big
sister was resentfully silent at first, but then,
from Second Auntie's strings of invectives, she
gained some idea of what had happened. At her
age, she already understood something of the
world and, surprisingly, began to feel welling up
in her feelings of joy as well as curiosity. Many
years later, she told my mother that before she
ever saw her, she had already begun to like this
woman who was able to make Second Auntie
lose her rag. Mrs. Shen, who had been forced
into joining the expedition, attended to the
needs of the four young ladies, together with
another maidservant. All the while, Mrs. Shen
racked her brains for a way to bring about a
peace. Second Auntie's brother had decided to
do his rounds among his broker acquaintances
right after his arrival in Shanghai, to find out
exactly where my parents lived and help his
sister raise hell. He was determined to do her
this service partly to consolidate her status
and partly because he was the one who had
started the fire, so to speak, and since he could
hardly back out of it now, he thought he'd

better stick up for her all the way to the bitter end. My second, third, and fourth sisters were too young to know anything. Nothing could have been more exciting than a train ride to Shanghai, which was even better than a spring outing to the suburbs. The three little girls noisily chased one another on the train in an exuberance of joy that was very much at odds with Second Auntie's mood. As a consequence, each girl got a series of slaps. As they wailed loudly, other passengers found them such a nuisance that they kept throwing Second Auntie poisonous looks.

After going through the exit of Shanghai's North Station, Second Auntie followed the advice of her brother and Mrs. Shen and divided the troops into two battalions. The first battalion consisted of her brother alone, with the mission of reconnaissance, to locate the target. All others were to march to Second Auntie's sister's home to await further orders after acquisition of intelligence information from her brother.

Second Auntie's brother soon found out my

mother's address. The broker he had sought
out for information was a slick character, one
who would not speak out of turn when not
asked, but when approached, he would not go
out of his way to guard other people's secrets.
Second Auntie's brother made a mental note of
the address. Knowing it was not far from where
he was, he decided, in a flash of inspiration,
to check the place out. He knocked on my
mother's door.

I have been told that it was I who went to
answer the door and that, before the visitor
spoke up, I said, all politeness, "Might you be
looking for Mr. Xuan, sir? He is not at home.
May I ask your honorable surname?"

Staring at me, a four-year-old boy at the
time, Second Auntie's brother involuntarily
broke into a smile. He saw my aquiline nose—a
distinctive feature of the Xuan family—and
noticed that my northern dialect had a hint of
the Anhui accent.

In the normal course of things, having
accomplished his reconnaissance mission, he
did not have to answer me. Or, he could have

come up with a lie and taken to his heels. He was a scheming and merciless man—I will come to that later, but that day, somehow I had cast a spell over him. Honestly, he replied, "My surname is Wen. I am from Suzhou."

With no idea what was happening, Mother came to the door with my brother, saying cordially, "Please come in!"

Second Auntie's brother suddenly remembered his mission. Before he even had a good look at my mother, he turned on his heels, saying, "No! No! Goodbye!"

In astonishment my mother watched the man beat a hasty retreat. I have been told later that, before my mother sensed any imminent danger, it was I who said with my ready tongue, "His surname is Wen. He's from Suzhou."

The sudden advent of a visitor named Wen from Suzhou gave my mother a bad feeling. My father never hid anything from her, so she knew that my father had never breathed a word about their Shanghai address to anyone of the Wen residence. As the saying goes, "He who has come, comes with ill intent." And

Father was away. As planned, he would be
arriving in Suzhou that very day from Weiting
and wouldn't be in Shanghai until the next
day. What was going to happen? My mother,
who had never experienced any kind of crisis,
did not have a clue, but she began to feel
apprehensive.

In the meantime, Second Auntie and her
foot soldiers were sitting solemnly in her sister's
home, waiting for news. Second Auntie's sister
was generous enough in material matters and
had given her husband's suit to my father, but
in this case, she had to follow usual practice
and did so more vehemently than Second
Auntie. She said that she would join her sister
and raid the love nest as soon as they obtained
the address. "Sister," she went on, "you give
that scoundrel Xuan a good lecture and let
me take on that shameless concubine who is
cheaper than a prostitute. The best way to deal
with such a concubine is to scratch her face
with all your ten nails and leave some trails of
color on her cheeks."

Second Auntie found the references to

"concubine" somewhat jarring to her ear, but her sister's righteous indignation touched her. After all, being a member of the Wen family, her sister was on her side, just as all Chinese were supposed to stand united against the Japanese aggressors. Second Auntie was not privy to her sister's secret. The truth of the matter was that Second Auntie's brother-in-law had recently got himself a concubine, a beautiful dancer of some repute at Paramount Dance Hall. However, with her legions of informers, Second Auntie's sister quickly learned all there was to know about her enemy before the honeymoon was over. With the method she had just taught Second Auntie, she ruined the face of that dancer and then, using her hefty private savings, calmed the storm by securing her enemy's promise to withdraw. The husband found himself a helpless bystander to the two women's fight and their subsequent deal. In the end, he went back to his wife, like a prodigal son returning home. Having resolved the matter, Second Auntie's sister saw no need to go public about it, but the hatred

for concubines had taken root in her heart and
had now found an outlet. In her momentary
rush of indignation, she forgot that her sister
was also a concubine.

As Second Auntie's brother-in-law listened
uneasily to his wife's oblique and veiled attacks
on himself, he felt sorry for my parents. He
was the only member of the Wen family who
was in the know about my parents' situation.
Although he was a journalist and my father a
merchant, they found themselves in tune with
each other. He had learned about my father's
secret by chance—he often visited a veteran
journalist who lived on Jinlong Street and
had happened to bump into my parents, but
it was entirely by his own decision to keep his
lips sealed about my parents' secret. Once he
said jocularly to my father, "If I had met such
a good woman, I would also have married her
without the slightest hesitation. Hey! I would
even have devoted myself entirely to her and
divorced that Wen woman!"

And now, when the same thing had
happened to him, he found himself in no

position to call the shots. As is the case with most men of letters, he was all words and no action.

Be all this as it may, one who works with his pen does have more tricks up his sleeve than the average man. While playing host to his sister-in-law, he searched for a way to help my parents out. At the first opportunity that presented itself, he slipped out of the house, dived into a small general store nearby, and asked a young apprentice there to deliver a note immediately to Jinlong Street. The note was as terse as an urgent telegram: "Woman Wen picking a fight. Flee."

My mother was debating with herself what to do about Mr. Wen's brief visit. This note was to her nothing less than an air-raid alarm. She fled Jinlong Street in a fluster, with me and my brother in tow. Without any relatives to turn to for help, she took us to the plank house at Sha Market where she and my father had lived when they first fell in love. The innkeeper remembered her, to be sure. Afraid of losing face, Mother lapsed into falsehood and said that a group fight on Jinlong Street frightened her, and that she was there to get out of harm's way. The innkeeper cordially asked us to stay for supper and promised to keep an eye on me and my brother if my mother wanted to go back to see how things stood.

A few hours later, my mother went home stealthily like a thief. No sooner had she turned onto Jinlong Street than she was detected by the neighbors who had gathered in groups of two or three. As they fixed on her their probing eyes, like so many searchlights, she knew that the Wens had been there and that her concubine status had come to light. Her legs began to tremble like cotton being fluffed. She took a deep breath and walked up to the house, painfully aware of the eyes glued on her. She had barely entered her door before she felt her whole body go limp. The wedding photo that had been hanging on the wall was now in pieces, scattered over the bed and the floor. All items of furniture in the two rooms were broken or flattened, looking as if Japanese soldiers had just done their dirty work there.

16

My Father, Second Auntie, and My Mother

If Second Auntie could have had her way, she would have waited for my mother to return so that she could fight her to the death. But she had brought along all the girls on this raid. Darkness set in, and the little girls were eager to go home, like little chicks pining for the nest. They clung to Mrs. Shen, screaming, grumbling, and sobbing. Trying to calm them down, Mrs. Shen kept saying purposely, "Oh, sweethearts, we'll be leaving in a minute. Be good and listen to your mom." She was hinting at Second Auntie that it was time to go.

Second Auntie's ransacking of my mother's

apartment did draw quite a crowd in the beginning. The neighbors gathered around and talked excitedly for quite a while. But, in the prolonged absence of the other party to the conflict, my mother, the dramatic effect of the event gradually wore off and the idle onlookers' interest in other people's troubles began to subside. Some of the older women remembered my mother's kindness and refinement, and the boys' good sense and weak constitutions. Their neighborly feelings quickly returned. There being no lack of sharp tongues in the alleys of Shanghai, someone in the crowd spoke up and, quickly, a volley of harsh words followed.

"So the place has been smashed up, and enough vicious things have been said. What's the point of her staying on?"

"Who knows? Maybe she's waiting for Mr. Xuan. What a thing to do, running after her man all the way to Shanghai!"

"Hee hee!"

"You can hardly blame Mr. Xuan. Look at the brood she's got! Every one of them will need a dowry. Why should the Xuan family line come to an end?"

More and more words, nastier still, flew at Second Auntie like bullets. She began to find them hard to stomach. These old Shanghai women certainly knew how to bully a stranger. They positioned themselves by the door and under the windows out of Second Auntie's line of vision, so that they could not be seen but only heard. Unable to find an adversary in the flesh, Second Auntie had to take the verbal abuses as passively as a boxer's punching bag. As for her brother, acting like the man that he was, he stoutly refused to get a piece of the action. Second Auntie's brother-in-law took his side and kept him at home. Second Auntie's sister had helped with smashing glass, tearing up photos, and hurling epithets at "that concubine," but all this agitation brought on an attack of stomachache. Clutching at her chest, she had gone to Renji Hospital. So Second Auntie gave up all thoughts of a protracted war. Under Mrs. Shen's urging, she eventually made an honorable retreat while keeping up a stream of curses.

While Second Auntie was in action, my father had just returned to his factory in Suzhou, escorting that wool-fluffing machine from Weiting. None the wiser about the fire in his own backyard, so to speak, he was surprised at the absence of his brother-in-law who was otherwise a fixture in his office, keeping a watchful eye on everything that went on in the factory. But quickly Father dismissed thoughts about his brother-in-law from his mind and busied himself with the assembling of the machine. By late afternoon it began to rumble. It was only after Father returned home, all tired out, that he learned from my half deaf and half mute grand uncle's mumbled syllables and agitated hand gestures that something had gone terribly wrong. Without a moment's delay, he ran to the train station to catch the next train to Shanghai.

He missed Second Auntie and her troops. As Second Auntie returned to the Wen residence, exhausted and the worse for wear, my father, livid with rage, flung open the door of his home on Jinlong Street, clenching his fists and gnashing his teeth, like a sharpshooter on the dueling ground, or a Spanish bullfighter, or a prisoner on death row on his way to the execution. The quietness so shocked him that he lost his breath and did not regain it for several moments. My brother and I were fast asleep in bed. Mother was sitting motionless amid the mess. The room was unlit except by a ray of faintly yellowish light from the streetlamp outside. My mother's face was deathly pale but tearless.

Father pounced on her. He checked her face, her neck, and her hands before making a dart for the two boys in bed. Finally realizing that no hand-to-hand combat had taken place, he heaved a deep sigh and sank on the edge of the bed. Throughout the evening, husband and wife did not exchange more than a few words. My mother lay curled up against my father, as if she had gone limp and her soul had been snatched away. As she lay in bed without really falling asleep, the slightest sound outside would frighten her into clinging more tightly to my father. Father did not have a wink of sleep throughout the night. Both of them were afraid that Second Auntie would sneak back for a second surprise attack. When they finally dropped off to sleep at dawn, the rumblings of night-soil carts over the cobblestone street woke them up. Holding my mother tightly in his arms, my father told her what he had in mind, "Let's move immediately. I'll stay with you. I will never go back to Suzhou again."

"That won't do," said Mother gloomily. "You've got a large family there. There's also the factory and your eldest daughter."

"I can't afford to worry about them!" replied my father. These bold words were hardly out of his mouth than there flashed before his mind's eye the little aquiline noses of his daughters and the wool-fluffing machine that had just been assembled and installed in his factory. He felt as if a blunt knife was cutting away at his heart.

Hurriedly my parents took me and my brother to Qiaojiashan, a small alley near Penglai Road in the South Market, and resettled there. The streets of that area were not straight but winding, forming a veritable labyrinth. Many of the streets and alleys even shared the same names. The War of Resistance against Japan having just ended, chaos reigned, especially in the recovered territory. My father had chosen this spot precisely because of its disorderly environment.

We took up the anteroom on the second floor, the best room in the entire old stone-gate brick *shikumen* building that was unique to Shanghai. However, because the faucet and the kitchen were downstairs, life was far less convenient than on Jinlong Street. My mother had to go up and down the stairs for the three daily meals and to fetch water for the washing needs of the family of four. At that time, she was pregnant with my sister and her footsteps were no longer as light and brisk as before. My memory of the year-long life at Qiaojiashan consisted mainly of Mother's footsteps on the wooden stairs.

My father was no longer "Boss Xuan." He was now a broker. He had used brokers' services in the past but he was now at the service of business owners. They called him "Old Xuan." Even though he knew Heavenly Bliss and Blue Lotus Pavilion inside out, he chose not to go there unless absolutely necessary. He made his rounds in the teahouses in the old section of South Market, where a broker could find a steady supply of modest commissions. Father not only resold wool at a profit but also dealt in silk, cotton, and other textile products, and, occasionally, resold a few antiquated machines. The commissions he made were just enough for the daily expenses of the family. But when mother was about to give birth to my sister, she refused to go to the hospital, saying that it was too expensive. She only hired a midwife in the neighborhood. Unfortunately, it was a difficult birth and the midwife lacked experience. My mother almost died. At his wits' end, Father called an ambulance and ended up paying several times more money.

The very purpose of our relocation was to hide from Second Auntie, so naturally Father would not give her our new address. As far

as Second Auntie was concerned, Father had
disappeared from the face of the earth. She
went to Shanghai, to Jinlong Street, to Blue
Lotus Pavilion and Heavenly Bliss, to her sister's
home and all the brokers whom she knew, but
finding him in such a large city was simply
out of the question. Worse still, Father had
purposely kept himself out of business circles
in the first few months and lived like a hermit
with us, mother and sons, off what private
savings he still had. None of his acquaintances
had any idea where he had disappeared to.
Second Auntie returned to Suzhou in a daze,
as if she had lost her senses altogether. Back
in the Wen residence, she smashed bowls and
plates and sought other vents for her anger. Big
Sister, of course, was the first victim. Thinking
that Second Auntie had gone too far, my deaf
and mute grand uncle rented a tiny wooden
cabin at the entrance of Stone Street and made
it a wooden-utensil repair stand. He and Big
Sister moved out of the Wen residence. How
could a small repair stand generate enough
income to pay for secondary-school tuition?

Big Sister had to drop out of school. Soon thereafter, Second Auntie took up opium smoking. All the male and female servants of the Wen family deserted her, leaving only Mrs. Shen to look after the three little girls. Second Auntie's brother ran Zhenxin Wool Mill but, being an accountant, he had little knowledge of technological matters and only managed to barely break even. A year later, with US wool products dumping into the Chinese market and no demand for Zhenxin's products, Second Auntie's brother took matters into his own hands and closed the factory.

While Second Auntie was unable to find my father, my father was well informed about the goings-on in his Suzhou home. The information came from Second Auntie's brother-in-law. He was the only one in the know about my parents' new home on Qiaojiashan, not the Qiaojiashan west of First Avenue but the Qiaojiashan in the old section of the South Market. When mentioning Second Auntie in her misery, Second Auntie's sister would heap curses on my father, which was how her husband got to learn about what went on in Suzhou. Sometimes he would say icily, "Didn't the whole thing get out of hand because you added fuel to the fire?" Sometimes he would say with emotion, "I never knew Xuan Zhigao was capable of such a gutsy move." These comments brought on attacks of stomach acid in his wife. However, Second Auntie's brother-in-law was, after all, not the kind that gloats over other people's misery. So every time he saw my father he would say, acting the peacemaker, "You can't leave such a big family in Suzhou to their own devices like this. Do some thinking. Maybe you'll come up with a plan that can let you have it both ways." These words stabbed Father's heart like so many knives. Every time after the two men met, Father returned home deathly pale, looking like a leaf of frostbitten spinach.

He hid nothing from my mother, and so she felt more troubled than he was. "Go take a look!" she said.

"If I do, I won't be able to come back here," countered Father.

"What's to be done?" My mother said with a sigh. "I feel sorry for your eldest girl."

"She's doing well in school," said Father. "She comes first in every exam."

"But I feel sorry for the three little ones as well. Mrs. Shen does have her hands full."

"I never expected the factory would come to this," said my father.

"Go take a look!" urged Mother. "You've given so much to that factory!"

"I can't afford to worry about it now," said Father with a sigh, his eyes staring vacantly into space.

After talking and sighing like this for several months, Mother, with more resoluteness than Father had ever given her credit for, went alone to the train station and bought a ticket to Suzhou.

"Go!" she said, carrying my month-old sister in her arms. "Just as your brother-in-law said, think of something that can let you have it both ways."

Part III

17

Big Sister and Second Auntie

Even a person as kind as my mother only hoped that my father could have it "both" ways, meaning he could take care of both his Shanghai home and his Suzhou home. Auntie Peach away in northern Anhui was the forgotten woman, as if she had nothing to do with the Xuan family and was a nonexistent illusion that belonged to another world, so it was only right that no one needed to give her a thought. Only one person yearned for the Number-One Mrs. Xuan as she took care of my grandfather and supported my big brother. That person was Big Sister.

At her first meal at the Wen residence,

Big Sister had left half a bowl of rice for her mother, so maddening Second Auntie that the woman ate half a bowl of rice less than usual. Five years later, at age fourteen, Big Sister acted went to Father's Zhenxin Wool Mill on her own initiative and worked for several days in a row among a group of temporary wool sorters. She sent every penny she made back to Anhui. She had reached puberty earlier than the average girl and, at age thirteen, was taller than Second Auntie. Now, wearing a face mask and mingling with the day laborers, she even fooled Second Auntie's brother, the accountant. Not knowing that it was already summer vacation, Second Auntie thought that Big Sister was going to school every morning, her satchel on her back. Of course Second Auntie would not stop her. It was on pay day when the day laborers were lined up to receive their wages that Second Auntie's brother recognized the "Number-One Young Mistress" among the payees. Second Auntie flew into rage upon hearing about this. With her vicious tongue wagging, my father also lost his temper.

"Don't you have enough food to eat and enough clothes to wear?" said Father. "If the neighbors get to hear about this, won't they laugh at the Xuan family? Imagine having a child working for wages at the family's own factory!"

Big Sister did not answer back, nor did she even look at my father. It was just as if his words had fallen on deaf ears. She understood, none better, the uniqueness of her status in the Wen residence. In her years of living there, somewhere between a maidservant and a "young mistress," she had learned to keep things to herself.

Second Auntie pressed the point. "If you really love being a laborer, you need not go to school next semester. You were just born to be a laborer!"

"Mother, have I ever let my grades suffer?" In authentic soft Suzhou dialect, Big Sister tossed a rhetorical question at Second Auntie. She had long acquired fluency in that dialect and was able to use its unique veiled sharpness to serve her purpose. She had consistently ranked first in school, year after year, had skipped two grades in a row, and had been promoted to secondary school after only four years of primary school. Attacking her on her education was the wrong tactic on Second Auntie's part. Angrily—the more so because she was in the wrong—Second Auntie said, "You may not have let your grades suffer but you've certainly let the household chores suffer! You may not have let your grades suffer but you've let the reputation of this family suffer! Who knows what you do with the money? You are too young to start preparing for your dowry! The Xuan family has raised a shameless hussy who subsidizes a lover! When are you going to bring your dashing young gigolo home and show him to us?"

If my father were not present, Second Auntie would have twisted Big Sister's arm or given her a slap across the face. Big Sister had certainly had more than her share of physical abuse. However, in the last six months or so, she had experienced a sudden spurt of growth and had become quite a big girl. Short and stocky Second Auntie had to raise her head to meet those black eyes that so resembled my father's. So Second Auntie had been laying hands on her less often. Moreover, my father, though a northerner, hated seeing children beaten. On one occasion, he flew into a rage when he witnessed Second Auntie spanking my fourth sister and wrested Fourth Sister away from her with such force that Second Auntie fell on the floor. Second Auntie knew this all too well and therefore tried her best not to ruffle my father's feathers. Without a vent for all her pent-up fury, she chose to resort to her rich supply of foul language to hurt Big Sister, letting her tongue run away with her to deal with this eldest Princess Xuan who, for some reason, she found a little intimidating.

Being accustomed to such outbursts, Big Sister listened with complete unconcern.

But Father found this torrent of words too much. "Hey!" he said. "What are you talking about? She is so young …"

"She may be young age-wise but she's certainly no child! She's making money off your factory to secretly support an outsider!"

Father was also bewildered. "My girl, what do you want to do with the money?"

Big Sister remained silent.

"Out with it!" Father raised his voice. "What on earth do you want to do?"

Big Sister raised her eyes and replied in an unadulterated Northern Anhui accent, "I have already sent the money to my mother, my grandfather, and my brother."

Father was astounded. Second Auntie fell silent. No one attempted to bother Big Sister anymore. Blithely she returned to the factory to resume her "work-study program" and worked for the whole summer.

One who hasn't done this can hardly imagine what a miserable job it is to sort wool in a factory in the summer. Using electric fans was out of the question, because the wool would be blown all over the place, and air-conditioning had yet to be invented. The sorters had to sit tight in the middle of piles of warm wool and try to ignore the wool that stuck to their sweaty skin. Even on the hottest

day, you had to wear a face mask, but even
with a mask, you still couldn't stifle a sneeze,
and your nostrils would itch so badly that you
would want to scrape off the skin. I'm able
to give this description because I have had
first-hand experience. It was summer when I
went to Father's factory to ask for tuition from
him. I saw with my own eyes perspiring wool
sorters with wool stuck all over their faces.
After sneezing more than twenty times during
my fifteen-minute stay with them, I could not
find the door quickly enough. But Big Sister,
at age fourteen, had worked there for a whole
summer!

She had planned on doing this again the
following year, but because Father had gone
into hiding for my mother's sake and Second
Auntie almost lost her mind for my father's
sake, Zhenxin Wool Mill soon closed down.
My grand uncle took Big Sister out of the
Wen residence and opened a repair stand on
Stone Street. The interruption in Big Sister's
schooling lasted nearly a year, during which
time she found odd jobs in various places

and sent to Anhui whatever money she had squeezed from a hand-to-mouth existence with my grand uncle. The three-member family in her home village thus had enough to survive the great famine in Northern Anhui in 1945 and 1946.

18

Big Sister and My Father

Father returned to Suzhou and became "Boss Xuan" again. Shaking up his factory under the restored name of Zhenhua was not a difficult job but putting the Wen residence in order was quite a struggle. Second Auntie having been smoking opium for several months, only the diamond ring she had bought after her wedding was left in the toilette box that she used for hoarding her private savings. She had a hard time trying to kick the habit. Every time the fit was on her, she would flop onto her bed, her face bathed in tears and nasal drippings, and bury herself in her quilt, wishing she could smother herself to death. As long as my father was with her, even if she felt more dead than alive, she would never beg for "a last puff," as some drug addicts do. Instead, she kept repeating to herself, as if cheering herself on, "I'm quitting! I'm quitting!" Having knocked about the business world for many years, Father had seen plenty of opium addicts and knew how tough it could be to try to kick the habit. Second Auntie's condition exasperated him but also, inevitably, saddened and moved him. Whenever he had a moment to spare from the factory, he willingly stayed with her, although less to wait on her and save her than to appease his conscience and redeem himself. The family misfortunes in the past year had made my ten-year-old second sister precocious. She not only helped Mrs. Shen with household chores but would also nestle against Father whenever the opportunity presented itself and whisper into his ears.

"Mother misses you. She looks at your photographs every evening!

"Dad, don't go. Mom said she would never go to Shanghai to smash glass again. My sisters and I won't ever go again, either!

"People say to me, your dad doesn't want you anymore. But that's not true, right?

"Dad, I miss Big Sister! She's making wonton in the wonton place on Stone Street. Please get her and grand uncle back!"

After Second Auntie got through the toughest two weeks of her struggle to kick her drug habit, Father invited my grand uncle back to the Wen residence and put the wool-fluffing machine under his care. My grand uncle thus became a full-time employee on regular pay. After Liberation, he married when in his fifties. He died of natural causes in the first year of the Cultural Revolution.

Big Sister, however, adamantly refused to go back to Quanfu Road.

Before Father returned to Shanghai, she had applied to a teacher-training school in Mudu Town in the far suburbs and had passed the entrance examination. It was a boarding school. When Father went to see her, she showed him the letter of admission and said, "I came second in the exam. The school provides free room and board for the top three students on the list, so I won't need your money."

Lost for words, Father gloomily finished smoking a cigarette before eventually speaking up, "It's been tough on you."

Big Sister made no response and kept herself busy packing her none-too-plentiful belongings. She was big of frame, like other members of the Xuan family, and looked from the back like an eighteen-or-nineteen-year-old girl. After a few moments of silence, she suddenly turned around and said with a radiant smile, "My … my mom in Shanghai is so beautiful!"

Caught off guard, Father stammered, "You … you've … you've seen her?"

From her small pile of clothing, Big Sister retrieved a photograph and handed it to Father. "Here! When they were tearing up photographs, I took one when nobody was looking and hid it on me. Both my two brothers look like you!"

When Father took the photo, his eyes misted over.

It was a five-inch enlarged photo of our family of four taken at Wang Kai's Portrait Studio when my brother was one year old. Mother was sitting on a chair with my brother in her arms. I stood leaning against her. Father, wearing a Western suit, stood by the chair with a serene and contented smile on his face. It was a heart-warming family photo. Upon my mother's request, the photographer added a light touch of soothing color on it, lending it the look of an elegant and unique watercolor portrait.

Later, Father told Mother that even though he had known early on that his oldest daughter would be the most outstanding member of the Xuan family, it was through this photo that he came to appreciate fully her maturity, her prudence, her magnanimity, and her thoughtfulness.

There was no need for negotiation or for written agreements. After having lived separately for more than a year, Father and Second Auntie reached a tacit understanding: As long as my father could come up with a reason to justify a business trip to Shanghai, Second Auntie would take it to be a genuine business trip and refrain from intervention. Thanks to his perseverance, Father won partial freedom as well as Second Auntie's acceptance of the fait accompli, and was able to "have it both ways," as he had hoped for.

Henceforth Big Sister never asked my father for money. Later Father learned that she had in her after-school hours tutored an eight-year daughter of a rich man in Mudu Town and not only paid her own way through school but also never stopped sending money to her home village in Anhui.

Big Sister also brought Father a windfall and gave a new lease on life to Zhenhua Factory when it was about to go under.

It was already 1948. Zhenhua Factory was hanging on to a miserable existence. It certainly did not look like it could ever regain its pre-war vitality. With neither the supply of raw materials nor the sales of the products going well, Zhenhua was like a pauper with just enough food to keep him alive. The wool-fluffing machine rumbled for only less than ten days out of a month and stayed idle the rest of the time. With prices soaring and the paper currency of 1948 worth less than toilet paper, Father found it harder and harder to support two families in two different locations. In spring of that year, Second Auntie, like an old tree bursting with blossoms, gave birth to my twin brother and sister. The twins were both a little retarded, as if by divine punishment for my father's attempts to "have it both ways," or probably because of Second Auntie's one-time opium addiction. They had enormous appetites with strong limbs and oversize heads but their eyes were always dull. In those days when even rationed rice was in short supply and had to be fought over, feeding the extra two mouths was like adding two mountains on my father's back. It was just too much for him. He was not yet forty, but his temples had turned gray.

One late night in the depths of autumn, Big Sister rapped on the gate of the Wen residence. Mrs. Shen, who opened the gate, saw a man standing behind Big Sister.

Father threw some clothes on himself and went to the main hall. Big Sister did not return home more than two or three times a year. At eighteen, she was quite a young woman with a graceful bearing and her independence had won the respect of everyone in the Wen residence, including Second Auntie. So upon hearing that Big Sister was there, Second Auntie also wanted to rise from bed. It was only after Father told her not to get out of the quilt and take away the warmth from the two little ones that she lay back in bed.

Without any prelude, Big Sister said to Father, "This is my teacher, Mr. Zhou. He's in a little trouble and would like to stay in the factory for a while to be out of harm's way."

With his quick mind, Father immediately understood the nature of the "trouble." The Communist troops had been gradually moving south. The Nationalist army, fighting a losing battle against them, had been frantically arresting civilians, many of whom had already been imprisoned or executed.

Correctly assessing the situation of the country, Father sensed the imminent demise of the Nationalist government and readily gave his consent. Moreover, Father saw immediately that Mr. Zhou the teacher was very likely going to be his son-in-law.

It was not a problem for Zhenhua Factory with its messy piles of wool and yarn to hide a person or two. Plus, Father was a longtime resident on Quanfu Road, known to the local headmen and the police station as "Boss Xuan," who, like most other business-owners, had no hand in politics. Mr. Zhou the teacher took off his Western-style shirt, changed into my grand uncle's tunic, and was installed in the factory with its large turnover of day laborers. As a result, he managed to throw his pursuers from Mudu off his trail. After the worst was over, Big Sister bought him a train ticket for Shanghai and escorted him to the train station.

Soon my father received a letter from him, saying he had set up a deal for my father and asked him to go quickly to Shanghai to close the deal.

Big Sister joined my father on the trip.

They met at mother's home. My mother had relocated again, this time to a small alley near Zhaofeng Park in the western part of the town. The place being far from the city center, the rent was very cheap and my mother did not have to share an exit with anyone, so she could avoid contact with the neighbors. For reasons of economy and privacy, Mother finally decided to relocate from the convenient downtown area to that factory zone with its forest of chimneys. In that dim and damp first-floor room, she met Big Sister for the first time.

"Mom!" Big Sister called her affectionately, even though she was only about ten years younger than my mother.

"Hello, Auntie!" said Mr. Zhou the teacher. An activist in the factories of the area, he was wearing a worker's overalls. Unshaven, he looked older than my mother.

While the two men talked business, the two women talked about me, my brother, and my sister. I distinctly remember how Big Sister

pressed our noses one by one with her soft and
cold finger. Then she laughed, covering her
mouth with a hand, and kissed us each on the
cheek with her soft and warm lips. I could tell
that she liked us. Some years later, I went in
desperation to Suzhou to look her up and ask
her for tuition for the three of us. My courage
came from memories of her finger and her
lips. I just knew that she would do her best to
help us.

Through Mr. Zhou, my father landed a
good deal. Mr. Zhou was in fact a Shanghai
rich man's son. His father owned a fairly large
shipping company with a pedicab department.
Mr. Zhou got my father the job of making
coarse woolen blankets for all the pedicabs
and rickshaws of the company. The blankets
were to cover the knees of customers in winter
and therefore did not demand high standards
for the quality of the wool or the weaving,
which could not have suited Father's factory
better. This job was like a shot in the arm to
the Zhenhua Factory when it was on its last
legs. It recovered and, while it was still busy

operating more than a year later in May, 1949, Suzhou and Shanghai were liberated.

We learned after Liberation that Big Sister had joined the Communist Party two years earlier, on Mr. Zhou's recommendation.

19

Auntie Peach, Second Auntie, and My Mother

Soon thereafter, the Marriage Law was widely publicized and was to be applied uniformly throughout urban and rural areas. Auntie Peach became a target of the local director of women's affairs.

"Xuan Zhigao is a polygamist. Why do you still hang on to him?" said the director. "The township government will help you divorce him."

"But why?" said Auntie Peach. "I get to live my life with or without him. I don't want to trouble the comrades of the township government."

"You made the list of 'poor peasants.' Make a clean break with him! Come on!"

"Haven't I done so already, long ago? I live with my father-in-law, who is also a poor peasant."

My grandfather and Auntie Peach had been grouped into the category of "poor peasants" during the land reform and even received some portable valuables once owned by a landlord of a neighboring village. As these were undeniable facts, the director of women's affairs was not able to change Auntie Peach's mind, and the conversation led nowhere.

It just so happened that Big Sister was in the village for a visit. Knowing my sister was also a government official, the single-minded director sought her out in the hope that my sister could talk Auntie Peach around. My sister replied with a smile, "In a case of divorce, the Marriage Law says it should be settled through voluntary consultation by both parties concerned. I as a daughter have no right to interfere."

By getting bureaucratic with the director,

my sister made her abandon the idea altogether.

The Women's Federation of Jinchang District, Suzhou, zeroed in on Second Auntie. A young woman about Big Sister's age, fresh out of school, paid a visit to the Wen residence, but, before she had finished making her point, Second Auntie launched into a speech that quickly silenced her.

"My dear girl," began Second Auntie. "I can see that you are not a longtime resident in the Chang Gate area. Why don't you take a walk down Quanfu Road and check with my old neighbors? Who doesn't know that Xuan Zhigao came here at age twenty, that he started his factory here, and that we held our fifteen-table wedding banquet here? My four daughters and one son were all born here. I don't care how many other wives he has. I, Wen Xiuzhu, am the only one who really lives with him! Of course the new society does not allow polygamy. Since Xuan Zhigao should have only one wife, I am all for his divorcing the other two and making this a one-husband-one-wife marriage as soon as possible! If you ask me, my dear girl, I suggest that you make two trips: the first one to Anhui, to talk that country woman into freeing herself from that arranged marriage and liberating herself, and the second trip to Shanghai, to tell that concubine that she is violating the Marriage Law and that if she refuses to divorce him, the people's government will deal with her according to the law. If you could accomplish these two tasks, my dear girl, not only will you win commendation from your office, but my whole family and I will be ever so grateful to you for your kindness!"

For all the deviousness of her argument and the harshness of her words, Second Auntie had the moral high ground. When the girl returned to her office and repeated Second Auntie's words to her colleagues in the Women's Federation, they did not know whether to laugh or get angry; and so, all of them washed their hands of Second Auntie.

All was well with my mother in Shanghai. The neighbors were not aware of the Xuan family's secret. They only knew that the man

of the family owned a small factory in Suzhou
and would naturally have to travel.

The secret nearly came to light later, because Auntie Peach took my oldest brother to
Shanghai.

My oldest brother had been of a weak
constitution since his earliest childhood. In
1952 when he was eighteen, he had not yet
reached puberty and looked like a twelve-or
thirteen-year-old boy. When Big Sister saw
him on her visit to her home village that year,
she immediately emptied all her pockets and
told her mother to take him to the county
hospital for treatment. But after the money had
all been spent, his condition still showed no
improvement. Watching young men of his age
getting married while he was still digging wild
water chestnuts in the pond, bare-bottomed,
my grandfather and Auntie Peach were sick
with worry. In the previous few years they were
too hungry to concern themselves with his
puberty problems, but now that life was better,
they were determined to get him medical
attention. My grandfather had a letter sent to

Big Sister. Unfortunately she was in Korea with a group entertaining the Chinese Volunteers and therefore did not receive the letter. After waiting in vain for a reply, Grandpa consulted Auntie Peach and, in the end, they wrote a letter to my father, first to find out what had happened to Big Sister and, secondly, to ask my father to make inquiries in the city about any treatment for my big brother's condition. Father took the letter seriously. Snobbery is a common human failing, and my father was no exception. A revolutionary cadre in the family was a source of pride. He now had someone to fall back on, and Big Sister was Auntie Peach's daughter. Things being no longer the way they used to be, he could not dismiss out of hand those members of his family in his home village. He took the letter to Shanghai and asked for my mother's advice. He did not let on any of this to Second Auntie because he knew her too well.

With her medical training, my mother concluded after reading the letter that my big brother was suffering from a kind of tuberculosis, known popularly as children's consumption. While my brother was in adolescence, immediate medical attention could affect a complete cure. My mother added, "There's no time to lose! Write a reply and tell Auntie Peach to bring the boy to Shanghai. The pulmonary department of Renji Hospital is internationally renowned. Quite a few of my former classmates are working there. I'll go ask for their help."

"Will that work?" Father hesitated. "Tuberculosis is contagious. What about our three little ones?

"I will quarantine him from them. Don't worry."

"But, what about Peach?"

"Nothing to it! I've thought everything out. I'll give the inner room to her and the boy. We'll take the outer room. It's summer, so we can bed down on the floor."

"I mean, what about the neighbors …"

"I've also thought about that. We'll just say that she is a cousin of yours and he is her son." Breaking into a smile, Mother continued,

"There is an element of truth to this, isn't there?"

She had always kept firmly in mind the whole series of legal procedures that she and my father had gone through before their wedding and had taken herself to be my grand uncle's daughter-in-law, a title she would comfort herself with at critical junctures.

Auntie Peach came, bringing my big brother with her.

My mother took him to Renji Hospital.

The doctors said that he had indeed had tuberculosis years earlier but it had calcified. His delayed development was due to tuberculosis plus years of malnutrition. With proper nutrition, his condition should turn for the better.

Auntie Peach and my big brother stayed in Shanghai for more than two weeks.

After installing Auntie Peach in Shanghai, Father began to steer clear of her—a policy he and my mother had settled on in advance. For the duration of their two-week stay, he was not to show his face again. Knowing my mother as well as he did, he went back to Suzhou without leaving a word of instruction, secure in the knowledge that Peach and her son were in good hands. So he busied himself with the factory until they were ready to go back to Anhui. As a courtesy, he came to Shanghai to send them off.

As it turned out, the chlorine-laced tap water of Shanghai upset Auntie Peach's stomach. Three days into her stay, she began to throw up and have bouts of diarrhea. Afraid that it might be something contagious, my mother changed rooms with my big brother, turning the inner room into a hospital ward with her as the nurse on twenty-four-hour duty. With her medical knowledge, she bought medicine from a pharmacy, made sweetened rice porridge, and put Auntie Peach on this semi-liquid diet until she quickly recovered from the disorder. During those few days, the room reeked with an offensive odor not unlike that of pungent vinegar because Auntie Peach kept throwing up whatever food she had eaten. Her intake of food was very limited but her bowel movements were frequent and incontrollable. As a consequence she had to have changes of underwear several times a day. My mother was kept so busy carrying back and forth the spittoon and the night-soil bucket and washing the patient's porridge bowls and underwear that she grew thinner by the day, but she never complained. She just did everything that she thought should be done, willingly and without ostentation, showing the patient endless consideration but doing it in a matter-of-fact way. After Auntie Peach had recovered and my big brother had been diagnosed, my mother took everyone on a trip to the city center, first to the City God Temple, then to the restaurant by the Zigzag Bridge for lunch. After we had eaten its famous steamed soup pork buns, we went to Big World Entertainment Center in the afternoon. My mother made us three children sit through two hours of an Anhui opera performance just to keep Auntie Peach and Big Brother company. We did not return home until after evening had set in, after having thoroughly enjoyed ourselves. In fact, my mother was quiet by nature and the last thing she liked was roaming the streets and joining the crowds.

Peach was a woman appreciative of kindnesses done to her, but, like my mother, she lacked Second Auntie's clever tongue. When she was ill, she did nothing more than tearfully hold my mother's hands, but after she recovered, she took up needles and thread and, with amazing speed, made one pair of cotton-padded shoes for each of the five members of our Shanghai family—all done within a matter of a few days and nights. I still remember those five pairs of shoes with their soles almost one inch thick and their uppers reaching all the way to the ankles. After I began to wear them, I was free of the frostbite that had tormented me every winter.

Now that I have learned everything there is to know about the Xuan family's secrets, I often think back on those two weeks when Auntie Peach and my mother got together for the first and last time in their lives. In trying to fathom their deep psyches, I believe that before they met, even though both were kindhearted women, they probably could hardly avoid being biased against each other, but those two weeks must have turned things around and led to a spiritual connection between them. They came to understand and appreciate each other. Upon learning about Auntie Peach's death a few years later, my mother lost no time in sewing a few black cloth armbands and made us wear them with her in mourning for a whole month. As for Auntie Peach, when she was about to board the train after her two-week stay in Shanghai, she suddenly turned around and said to Father, there to send her off as a matter of courtesy, "You've got yourself a wonderful wife! Don't you ever leave her!"

Father did not know whether to laugh or cry at this last-minute advice before she left. Auntie Peach sounded more like his mother than his number-one wife.

20

My Father and I

I completed my second year at junior secondary school in 1955. In the summer, I went for the first time to Suzhou, to ask my father for my tuition for the next semester. As I entered Zhenhua Factory, with the profits of which my father supported his families, I was surprised by what I saw. I had never thought that the food for the more than ten members of the two families had come from this dilapidated one-story structure with its swirling dust and ear-splitting noise. Wearing a tank top and an almost threadbare pair of pants, with wool covering up his head and his whole body, Father was standing by a tiny window and staring at some wool he was holding in his hand, totally unaware of my presence. He was only forty-four or forty-five that year, but his vision had already blurred with age. He was holding that handful of wool at full arm's length and squinting at it as if taking aim at a target. I called out, "Dad!"

He did not hear me. I cried again at the top of my voice, trying to compete with the roaring wool-fluffing machine. Only when I unceremoniously poked him in his side did he discover me.

Later I understood why Father lost much of his hearing so early in life.

But my father proudly took me on a tour of the factory. Of course I was able to feel his pride in parading me around because of my strong resemblance to him. I remember how awkward, shamed, and impatient I felt at the time. Father had no inkling of the stigma that I had subconsciously attached to my lineage. I forced myself to follow him, feeling as if crushed by the rumbles of the machines, and I kept sneezing from the dust, wool, and the

stench of sheep that filled the air. The smiles
of my deaf-mute grand uncle, the iciness of
Second Auntie's brother, and the sharp glares
of the women sorters all made me feel as if
they were saying, "Oh, so this is the son of that
concubine in Shanghai!"

With that line buzzing in my ears, I
paid no attention to my father's proud and
professional narration about the factory. Only
when I entered the large workshop with three
large carpet-weaving machines did I draw a
long sigh of relief, because there, the wool-
fluffers' rumbles were partially blocked by the
wall and the nauseating stench of sheep was
less offensive. There was no one else in the
workshop.

Rubbing his hands, Father said, "This batch
of wool hasn't been dyed. So the workshop has
to stay idle while waiting for dyed wool. Once
it's in operation, it's quite a lively place."

In high spirits, he went up to one of the
three machines and gave me a demonstration
of the manual operations that I have described
earlier. They were manual operations, pure

and simple.

"Who usually works in this workshop?" I could not resist asking.

"Myself, your grand uncle, and your second and third sisters. Your third sister was among the sorters you just passed. She's also on summer vacation. After operation in this workshop begins, those in the front will move here. Sometimes we also hire day laborers."

I was only fifteen at the time, but, being a resident in a factory zone in the western part of Shanghai, I knew that Zhenhua had none of the look of a regular factory. Any decent factory should have a never-ending flow of operations. There certainly should be no breaks in between, with the same group of workers moving back and forth. I finally realized, with my eyes bearing witness, that after struggling for decades, my father's factory was still, to say the best, no more than a handicraft workshop.

I asked Father for tuition for the three of us children for the next semester.

Father kept rubbing his hands, rolling the wool dust and his sweat into long strips that fell to the floor like so many worms. As if suffering from toothache, he made hissing sounds and said without looking at me, "Haven't I just sent money to your mother?"

"That was just to put food on the table," I said. Every member of the Xuan family, except my big brother, was precocious. I had begun helping my mother keep the family account book at age twelve.

"How many days before school starts?" asked Father, throwing uneasy glances at Second Auntie's brother's office. Obviously he was afraid that someone might be eavesdropping.

"The day after tomorrow. Otherwise, Mom wouldn't have told me to come."

In fact, Mother didn't tell me to go to Suzhou, but she had lost the argument with me and had reluctantly given me enough money for the round trip. Time and again, she had cautioned me, "Don't push him too hard. Your father is in a difficult position. Second Auntie keeps tight control over him, and there are the two retarded little ones with their big appetites. Your father is having a hard time trying to take care of so many people."

Giving her a withering look, I said, "Who should I look to if not him? Why did he choose to have us in the first place?"

My mother broke down in tears. My surliness with Mother was a result of her pampering me. In my father's presence, I would never bring myself to say such harsh things. Even though he was sleeveless and covered with dust, he still had an air of authority, for whatever reason, so that at that age, I shrank back from defying him. So I had to hide under my mother's umbrella and stretch the truth a little by saying that she had told me to make the trip. Amid the rumbling of the machine, I heard my father heave a long, drawn-out sigh.

"Many bills are due for payment," he said, "but I haven't been able to collect the payables. And the wages for the day laborers are also due. Also, your fourth sister is in the hospital ..."

For the first time, I saw signs of aging on his face.

For the first time, I eagerly offered him an idea. "Maybe you could take me to Big Sister."

Gasping with realization, he said, "Yes! Let's go to your sister!"

I was confident. I remembered her pointed finger and her warm and soft lips, and I knew that she was now a vice bureau chief.

21

Second Auntie, My Mother, and Big Sister

In 1956, Zhenhua Factory became a part of Suzhou State-owned Carpet Factory. Because Zhenhua's assets had exceeded twenty million in the old currency and because Father had hired two regular employees—my grand uncle and Second Auntie's brother, Father was put into the category of capitalists. Soon, Zhenhua Factory became a raw material warehouse for the state-owned factory. My father, my grand uncle, and Second Auntie's brother now had to go by bus to the eastern part of the city for work every day. My father became a technician in charge of wool blending. According to the

government's policies for industrialists, once
their businesses merged with state-owned
businesses, they were put on government
payroll and their spouses, if they wanted,
could also be employed and stand on their own
two feet. Right away, Second Auntie began to
work for Suzhou Carpet Factory as keeper of
the Quanfu Road Warehouse. My second and
third sisters also took the offer and became
regular wool textile workers. My fourth sister
was still a student at a teacher-training school
and, in her off-school hours, looked after the
house. Mrs. Shen had passed away. The twins
were doing badly in primary school and often
had to repeat the same grade. Whichever way
you look at it, there were more people in the
Wen residence working and drawing salaries
than those needing support, and therefore
they were having a pretty easy time of it.

However, the four of us in Shanghai had
fallen on hard times. My father was now
drawing a monthly salary with no other
income. Should his only source of income fall
under someone else's control, he would lose all

room for maneuvering. Second Auntie was now working with him in the same factory. On every payday, she invariably signed for both their salaries. With her chubby fists watertight, she did not allow Father to have enough pocket money for a train ticket to Shanghai, although she did provide my father with food and drinks, and smoked Flying Horse cigarettes together with him. In addition to presentable reasons such as, she as the mistress of the house needed to keep expenses within their limited income, to make large plans for the whole family, and to make every penny count, there was also a deeper reason for her behavior—a reason that every member of the Xuan family knew but did not want to give voice to. And that was her deep-seated hatred for my mother. A woman can never forgive another woman who steals her man. With her background as Miss Wen, daughter of the local bully, with her shrewdness and ability, she had, amazingly enough, been stooping to compromise for more than ten years, playing dumb, letting my father "have it both ways," and asking for only a modest share of him. This was certainly not her idea of what her life should have been, but she had simply had no other choice. As soon as the right time had come, she would go to any lengths to turn her defeat into victory, oust my mother, an intruder, and regain my father. And now, the opportunity had presented itself. She was no longer wife of Boss Xuan. In the state-run Suzhou Carpet Factory, she was the fit and proper Mrs. Xuan, wife of Xuan Zhigao, fully entitled to taking two salary payments on paydays. No one in the factory raised any objections. Even those who knew that my father had another family would not poke their noses into what did not concern them. Father, in his anxiety to keep up appearances, hated to bring family quarrels into the open, and so he suffered in silence. He did try a few times to put up a fight. He cursed, he smashed a few bowls, he even raised his hand against Second Auntie, but nothing worked. My second, third, and fourth sisters all took their mother's side.

"Everybody should work for a living!" said my second sister.

"There are three members of this family who need support. Don't you have a responsibility toward them?" said my third sister.

My fourth sister, being the best educated of the three, reasoned with Father in these words, "Explain everything clearly to my Shanghai mother. If she really can't hold out any longer, why don't you agree to a divorce, so that she can find another man to support her?"

Without missing a beat, Second Auntie said magnanimously, "If so, I'll take the three children in Shanghai. They can have the household registration authorities grant them a change of domicile and relocate to Suzhou. I will support them, just as I supported Big Sister!"

The three sisters burst into a chorus of cheers.

Thus besieged, Father met a crushing defeat, as was only to be expected.

Economic control meant restrictions on movements. As an employee now, Father had to go to work every day, so he lost his freedom, and the slenderness of his means deprived him of all courage to come to Shanghai and see us. In the first half of 1958, he was absent for four months in a row, nor did he make a single remittance. Mother wrote him one letter after another and got in response nothing more than a brief note saying he was well. Containing only about a dozen characters, it was as terse as a telegram.

We began to make ends meet by making frequent trips to the pawnshop. I was seventeen, my brother fifteen, and my sister twelve. Our three hungry mouths quickly forced the sale of all the valuables at home. My mother had no financial sense and had never put aside any private savings or planned a way out for herself. She had wholeheartedly attached herself to my father. Now that the big tree had fallen, she found herself helpless. What time she had to spare after taking care of the three of us, she spent in shedding tears and heaving sighs without the least idea what to do. During those six months, whenever she heard footsteps approaching the door, she would stop whatever she was doing, freeze, and listen with cocked ears like a rabbit. Only after the footsteps had disappeared again would she let out a breath. When summer arrived, she suddenly had to be hospitalized for a gastric hemorrhage. I took matters into my own hands and sold off the only expensive piece of furniture in our home—the large mahogany bed that she shared with my father, and paid up her hospital bills. With the balance of the money, I bought a new single bed with a nice new wooden frame strung with crisscross coir ropes. But after she was discharged from the hospital and saw the new bed, she broke down in a flood of tears.

She wrote a letter to Big Sister.

My mother had obtained her address by barging into the Shanghai Federation of Trade Unions building, where she found Mr. Zhou the teacher—now chief of the Federation's Department of Outreach. We had all thought that Big Sister was going to marry him, but that didn't happen. After Liberation, Big Sister had first joined a land reform task force and then she spent more than a year in the battlefields of Korea. When I made that trip to Suzhou, she had just been promoted to vice chief of the Suzhou Textile Bureau. Her husband was an official from the north. A big Northeasterner, he was far less handsome than Mr. Zhou. My mother had asked my father what had gone wrong, since Big Sister had been in love with Mr. Zhou and the two of them would make a very nice couple. Father told her that Mr. Zhou already had a wife, although it was an arranged marriage, and that Big Sister had refused to be with him because of this. As soon as the words were out of his mouth, Father began to regret them. Mother also was caught between tears and laughter, and stopped comparing my brother-in-law to Mr. Zhou. Big Sister had moved several times. Not knowing her address, my mother had thought of Mr. Zhou and, unexpectedly, managed to obtain the address from him.

Big Sister escorted Father to us as if marching a prisoner-of-war.

At twenty-six, Big Sister looked spruce and smart with her bobbed hair, her Russian-style double-breasted blazer with its narrow waist, and her snow-white blouse collar over the lapels of her platye. Although she also had an aquiline nose, due to its right size and proportions it looked straight and pretty on her oval face. Her black eyes were unusually bright and never shifted when looking at people. No sooner had she entered the room than she called out in her crisp voice, "Mom!" Before even uttering a word, my mother dissolved in tears.

Big Sister who was now a vice bureau director said, "It's an easily solvable problem made complicated by you! I've already talked with your Suzhou family and told them not to be so highhanded. They should be more reasonable. I've struck a deal with them. From now on, Dad's salary will be divided into two portions, one for the Suzhou family, and one for the Shanghai family. Dad has responsibility toward both, and whichever family he is with, pays for his food. On the four Sundays of a month, Dad can go to whichever family he wants. No one has the right to interfere."

Father listened with bent head to what sounded like a court decision, whereas Mother kept nodding in agreement.

"Mom," continued Big Sister, adopting a very mild tone, "As I see it, the three little ones have grown up. You shouldn't always treat them as if they were still children. Why don't you go out and look for a job? If you have some money of your own, your fate won't be in other people's hands. Don't you agree?"

Mother said meekly, "I do want to find a job, but where can I go to look for one? I don't even know where these places are."

Smilingly, Big Sister said, "Mom, didn't you courageously go to the Federation of Trade Unions? Go there again and look for Old Zhou. The Xuan family saved his life. He will think of a way."

Having said this, Big Sister's face broke into an extraordinary, radiant smile. Once I had grown into adulthood, I understood that the radiance of that smile came from the generosity of her being. That day, my little brother and sister were both away in school but I was at home, studying for the college entrance exam, and therefore got to witness what I had described above. Standing by my mother's side, I was overwhelmed with admiration for this big sister who had so efficiently solved a complex problem. If I had an idol in that period of time, it wasn't any hero or movie star, but Big Sister.

22

Big Sister and Auntie Peach

Big Sister had to rush back to Suzhou that very day. So I took her to the train station.

She asked me, "I heard that you sold their bed?"

"Yes. I thought Dad would never come back again."

Big Sister burst into a peal of laughter. Pointing at the tip of my aquiline nose, she said, "Look at you! You are too young to know better!"

Being already half a head taller than she was, I felt quite embarrassed at being thus treated in public by a woman, but I also found myself happier than words could describe.

Again I was conscious of my sibling bond with her. When passing a fruit stand at the train station, Big Sister suddenly stopped in her tracks and exclaimed, "I had no idea Dangshan pears were available in Shanghai so early in the season. This kind of pear is delicious. It comes from Anhui!"

I made no response. We had been in straitened circumstances for years. Mother rarely bought fruit, especially fruit that were just in season. Big Sister gave me an intent look before she walked up to the fruit stand and picked up the largest pear.

"Are you buying just one?" asked the peddler.

"Yes. It probably weighs more than a catty?"

"You are a good judge of weight. It's a catty and two *liang*."

"Do you have a knife? May I use it?"

Big Sister began to peel the pear. When she finished, the peel still clung loosely to the pear without falling off. Then she lifted the peel and handed me the pear.

"Try it! This is an unusually large pear. I guarantee that you will never forget the taste!"

I never did forget the taste. I also kept in mind what she had said to me at the ticket booth, losing her smile, "Don't do as Father did!"

It's small wonder that she was resentful against Father, for all her wisdom, her magnanimity, and her aptitude for reading people's feelings. She, more than anyone else, understood the causes leading to Father's tragedy and empathized with Father in his awkward position. In her objectivity, she also knew full well that Father was not the only one to be held responsible for such a situation. However, the burden Father had shifted on her was way too heavy for her. Father should have shouldered the burden alone, but he was not up to it and transferred all of it to her. She couldn't do otherwise than feel exhausted, wronged, and resentful. Later I learned that she had not only sent much-needed money to Anhui through her labor at age fourteen, but for decades after she began to draw a regular salary, she had never stopped supporting my grandfather, Auntie Peach, and my big brother as they struggled for a living on the barren land. She even paid for the betrothed gifts for my big brother's prospective wife after he had belatedly reached puberty. In addition, I learned that not only her Anhui family, but our siblings in the Wen residence of Suzhou also took her to be Guanyin Bodhisattva, the Goddess of Mercy, and made a habit of going to her by turns to pour out their woes to her and ask her for help, even though she had children of her own and had her share of stress. For the sake of the family bond, she did not have the heart to turn them down, but if everybody takes a bite at a pear, however large it is, only the bitter core will remain. Knowing this full well, my mother told the three of us children in Shanghai to refrain as much as possible from asking Big Sister for help. Still, after learning that I had passed the college entrance exam, Big Sister made a remittance right away, specifying on the remittance form that the money was for books, miscellaneous

fees, and clothes. When I came upon the last
word, I realized that she must have noticed the
two big darns on my pants when I was seeing
her off at the train station.

Acting on Big Sister's advice, my mother
paid another visit to Mr. Zhou, after which
our neighborhood committee received a
phone call from the Federation of Trade
Unions. My mother was then given a job in
the neighborhood health center, where she
was to give injections and dress wounds. The
income was not much, but it was better than
nothing. More importantly, at least we didn't
have to make trips to the pawnshop if Father
missed a payment.

The great famine of Anhui in 1960 came
unexpectedly, both to the Great Leader and
the common people. Not much time earlier,
the Xuan Family villagers were eating their
fill from the communal pot and enjoying
"Communism." And then, amid the cheers
of "raising production sky-high," the supply
of grain came to an abrupt end. Big Sister
saved ten catties' worth of grain coupons per

month from her family's food provisions and unfailingly sent them to Anhui but they could only last a few days each time. My grandfather sent a letter to my father, appealing for urgent help. Letters from my grandfather were few and far between, about once every few years, so Father knew that his proud father would never speak up asking for help unless it was absolutely necessary. Without a moment's delay, he gave the letter to Second Auntie. Playing the good wife and mother at this critical moment, Second Auntie forthwith produced twenty catties' worth of national grain coupons as a contribution to the Xuan clan. But in his haste, Father sent by regular rather than registered mail the small sheet of coupons that could make the difference between life and death. Somewhere along the route, some scoundrel must have intercepted the letter. It was never delivered. Father didn't realize his mistake until a few days later when he received another letter, this time written in dire despair. As there was no way to redress this mistake, Father had no alternative but to go to Shanghai for help. By that time, Shanghai had also fallen on hard times, with green and stone hard outer cabbage leaves making up the bulk of the three daily meals of the residents. (To this day, I still haven't figured out why cabbages at that time grew only hard outer leaves and had no tender hearts.) Even so, my mother took out fifteen catties' worth of grain coupons from her grain ration book, went with Father to the post office, and sent them by special registered mail. While the grain coupons were on their way, Auntie Peach ate some white clay to stay her hunger and died.

Big Sister went to her home village for the funeral without asking Father to go along. He did want to go, but Big Sister asked, "Do you think you should?" The question was brief but the implication was all too clear. My father had to drop the idea.

With her status as a "poor peasant" and the mother of a revolutionary cadre, Auntie Peach got to be buried in the piece of land on the sunny slope at the eastern end of the village. After a few years, my grandfather was also buried there.

Later, when Big Sister talked with me about her mother's death, tears still welled up in her eyes.

"She didn't have to die," she said. "She had more grain in stock than others, but there were not necessarily deaths in those other families. She refused to eat, always wanting to save some food so that it could last longer and sustain them until our coupons arrived. We were too late in sending the coupons, and her starvation lasted too long. Two weeks before she died, she gave the grain to Grandpa and the others whereas she herself filled her stomach with cooked wild water chestnuts from the pond, tree barks, and grassroots. Your big brother's wife was a bad one. She walked off with all the grain coupons and money of the family and eloped with a carpenter of the same village. The good and the bad are not divided along the gender line, but there are more women than men who place other people's interests above their own, put up with hardships to help others and sacrificed themselves for the sake of their loved ones. My mother was such a woman."

Big Sister said this to me alone when I was in her home. Her tone was quite different from the tone she adopted when she was in her office. When I saw her in her office, I found her an entirely different kind of person, offering no such observations on human nature that deviated from class theory.

23

My Father and Second Auntie

In the Cultural Revolution, every member of the Xuan family, old or young, came to be denounced as a "demon."

My father was the source of all evils. After his trip to Anhui in the spring of 1966 for my grandfather's funeral, he lost all the blessings of his "poor-peasant" ancestors. The very next day after his return to Suzhou, the "Four Clean-ups Movement" task force of the carpet factory summoned him and suspended him from his post in order to have him confess his wrongdoings. His wrongdoings were of an economic nature. The one who denounced him was his close relative and director of the accounting office—Second Auntie's brother.

What had happened was that beginning from 1963, taking advantage of the relaxation in government policies, my father talked a production brigade in Weiting (where he had set up a workshop) into starting a workshop to process raw material for wool mills in Suzhou and Kunshan. It was back-breaking work but the profit margin was quite decent. After two or three years, the cash value of the production brigade's work-points [units indicating the quantity and quality of labor performed in rural people's communes as basis for payment—translator] shot up from less than a yuan to more than three yuan per day per point. With his many connections in the wool industry and his expertise, Father did a great deal for the founding of the workshop and its daily operations, which was why, from time to time, he received gifts of rice, pork, fried tofu, mungbean noodles, rice cakes, and whatnot. On festive occasions, when the production brigade paid out bonuses, Father also accepted red envelopes containing money.

After intense investigations and verifications, the "Four Clean-Ups" task force concluded that within a space of three years, my father had been guilty of taking agricultural and side-line products worth 1,500 yuan at the market price and five red envelopes containing 500 yuan in total, thus adding up to 2,000 yuan, just enough to be convicted of a crime. And so he was declared guilty of economic crimes, someone who ran an "underground factory" to "chip away at the edifice of socialism." Now that he was branded a criminal, he was to be put under surveillance. Straightaway he was transferred from the technical department to the loading docks to work as a stevedore.

In all fairness, Second Auntie's brother's denunciation of my father did not deviate from the truth, and the "Four Clean-Ups" task force, complying with government policies of the time, did not go too far in concluding that my father was "obstinately taking the capital-ist road." To this day, I still acknowledge that my father did pursue "capitalism" all his life. I still recall how Father radiated with energy in

those three years, busying himself with starting
and running a small wool workshop that lent
meaning to his life. He was in his fifties but he
had none of the withered and tired look appar-
ent in his forties. In my memory of those three
years, he was always on the go. With the zipper
of his jacket always open and a black imitation
leather bag in hand, he would rush to Shanghai
to stay for a few hours and leave in a hurry after
a meal with us, saying that since he had seen
us on a Sunday morning, his only day off, he
must devote the afternoon to the workshop in
Weiting. "A shipment of wool has just arrived,"
he would say. "I have to go and check the quality." His zippered imitation leather bag was
always filled to bursting with strips of wool.
Sometimes he went to Weiting first and arrived
in Shanghai in the afternoon, most often carrying a large bag filled with rice cakes, mungbean
noodles, and bags of soybeans and mungbeans,
and the savory aroma of home-made fried tofu
filled the air. Ah, even I, assistant professor of
history kept on by my university after gradua-
tion, also enjoyed plenty of the goodies my fa-

ther brought home by taking the capitalist road.

As a consequence, Father got all of us in trouble. His two wives became spouses of the enemy under surveillance, and all of us siblings, children of the enemy. This is why I said earlier that Grandpa and Auntie Peach had died at the right time. A little later, and they would not have qualified for the sunny slope at the eastern end of the village.

As soon as the Cultural Revolution started, Father became a major target for denunciation. His capitalist status plus his illegal underground factory qualified him as a fully-fledged class enemy. After a few months of the denunciation, two groups of people from Shanghai descended on him almost at the same time. The first one was from Second Auntie's brother-in-law's newspaper. Newspapers were not immune to "rebels," of course. The old journalist had also become a target. Actually, he himself was partly to blame. As he got on in years, he grew increasingly fond of blowing his own trumpet. On every possible occasion he would bring up his erstwhile membership at the Leftist League and his imprisonment by the Nationalist Party, to show that he had been a leftist very early on. To his dismay, questions arose: If he had been imprisoned, how did he get out? Chiang Kai-shek had famously said, "Far better to kill a thousand unjustly than let a single one slip away." So how did he manage to slip away? Vigorous investigations were made. In Suzhou, the investigators jumped in horror when they learned that my father had a connection in the Nationalist Party's Shanghai Garrison. For purposes of further investigation, they lost no time in confining my father to a small warehouse of shuttles, where the fleas and mosquitoes enjoyed him for more than a month.

The other group had impressive backgrounds and came from the Shanghai municipal government. By the time they arrived in Suzhou, Father had already taken up quarters in the warehouse. So the interrogation took place on site.

"How are you related to him?"

"He was my daughter's teacher. I was a

parent."

"Didn't you know that he was a traitor? Out with the truth!"

"Traitor? I don't think he has ever been imprisoned."

"Silence! Do we need you to pass judgments on the case? Confess! From November to December of 1948, what counter-revolutionary activities did the two of you engage in?"

"In those two months, he was helping out in my factory to stay out of harm's way. At the end of the year, he got me a deal …"

"Aha! Helping a capitalist exploit workers! If this isn't typical of his class, what is? He's the son of a capitalist to begin with!"

After visits from these two groups of people, political problems were added to my father's list of economic crimes. The factory assigned a special group of investigators to his case. The investigators took one trip after another to Shanghai for his case and, while they were at it, they bought in Shanghai cheap but good things and hauled them back to Suzhou. However, my father's life of isolation did not last long, because the man watching him could not stand the bugs, mosquitoes, flies and fleas of the warehouse anymore.

Often in life it is difficult to say if something should be regarded as a blessing or as bad luck. Due to poor health, Mother took early retirement from the neighborhood health center only one month before the outbreak of the Cultural Revolution in 1966. Just as she was about to go through with the retirement formalities, she became upset over twenty to thirty yuan she would lose each month. I tried to cheer her up by saying that since my brother was also about to graduate from college, we would support her until the end of her days, that if only she could take good care of her health, she would be able to enjoy boundless good fortune later in her life, and that if her health broke down, she would not be able to enjoy anything. Only then did she make up her mind to retire. Had she remained in the health center, she would have come to greater grief.

But she was implicated, after all. One day, when she was alone at home, several Red

Guards speaking the Suzhou dialect and wearing red armbands barged in. Mother realized
that this was a raid. Her legs gave way under
her and she plopped down on the edge of the
bed. Her face was probably deathly pale, which
may be why the Red Guards dared not lay a
hand on her. One of them barked a few questions at her, but her lips trembled so violently
that she couldn't get a word out. We didn't have
even one decent-looking piece of furniture.
On the table was laid the meal that my mother
had just cooked: a bowl of eggplants, a bowl
of baby bok choy, and a saucer of fermented
tofu. No drawer or cabinet was locked. The
articles of clothing that they pulled out of the
drawers were clean and neatly folded but were
either darned or threadbare. The "rebels" finally retrieved from the bottom of a trunk the
marriage license bearing my grand uncle's seal
and the family photo saved by Big Sister. They
took both items, saying they had enough to
show the decadent lifestyle of capitalists.

Luckily we lived on the first floor and had
the exclusive use of a door that led to the

outside. Luckily Mother was now a housewife without a job. So this raid did not catch the attention of any of our neighbors.

Big Sister was less lucky. She was denounced as a "capitalist roader," with a capitalist family background, as proven by my father's status. In the scorching heat of August, 1966, I went to Suzhou in an attempt to submit a petition for divorce on behalf of my parents. To my horror, I saw Big Sister on the plaza in front of the train station. Sandwiched between two large posters filled with writing, wearing a tall paper hat and only one shoe, she was being paraded by a group of male and female Red Guards on a makeshift platform as a "demon." I recognized her when I was still a good distance away. Without realizing what I was doing, I pushed through the crowd all the way to the foot of the platform. As I raised my face to look at her, I noticed that the brown paper hanging in front of her chest had been driven into her shoulders with a few thumbtacks. Blood was oozing around them. Underneath was written in large characters in heavy black ink:

"Born to a reactionary capitalist, a capitalist roader, mistress of the head of Shanghai's Scab Union …"

I did nothing to wipe away the tears and the sweat all over my face. My feet seemed to be rooted to the spot.

In a flash, Big Sister, with her head sunk on her chest, saw me. I don't know how a person's eyes could shine with such intensity under glaring sunlight. Her eyebrows tightly knit, she fixed her penetrating eyes on me for a few seconds before sweeping them to the other side of the platform. Guided by her eyes, I saw that, among the group of people wearing red bands, stood Second Auntie's brother! He was already in his forties, yet he wore a Red Guard band on his arm. In those years, class transcended kinship. Back in 1956 when Zhenhua Factory merged with the state-run factory, he had been classified as an employee exploited by my father, and after the "Four Clean-Ups Movement," he further disassociated himself from my father. I understood Big Sister's anxiety. Giving a wipe to my face, I slipped out of the crowd.

At the gate of the spacious, brightly-lit and orderly state-run carpet factory, I saw my father at work, moving toward a truck with a full sack of yarn on his bent back. At his height, the sack reached the baseboard of the truck. Two young workers lifted the sack from his back and piled them up. Relieved of the burden, he heaved a sigh, pulled down the hemp bag over his shoulder that served as a pad, and wiped off the sweat on his face. The dirty and tattered bag looked like a lama's cassock when draped over his shoulders.

I made a dart toward him and called out, "Dad!"

He was startled. "Why are you here?"

I didn't dare to state the purpose of my trip at that moment. How could I deal a blow on those shoulders that had just been relieved of a sack of yarn weighing more than a hundred catties? I had brought with me my mother's power of attorney and a petition for divorce signed by her. The purpose of my trip was to press him into going to the court and completing the divorce procedures. Knowing what a blow this could be for my fifty-odd-year-old father, I immediately decided to abandon the same-day return ticket and stay for one night, so as to soften the blow somewhat.

I helped him carry a few sacks of yarn. I was just as tall and big as my father, but even at my age, I found it quite a tough job. The two young men on the truck merrily slapped me on the shoulder. One said, "You must be Old Man Xuan's son in Shanghai. Your aquiline nose tells the whole story!"

The other put in, "I've been to your home in Shanghai in a raid! My goodness, your mother was a looker when she was young! We brought back a family photo of yours and hung it on the class struggle exhibition of the factory. It drew big crowds!"

"We heard that you are a college professor? Hey! Why would a big fellow like you want to stay a stinking intellectual?"

After my father's shift was over, I followed him back to the Wen residence.

This was the first time I saw the inside of that house. With her head half shaved as a sign of humiliation by the Red Guards of the block, Second Auntie was busily cooking supper. With all due respect, I called her "Mother." She stood immobile, at a loss as to how to react. As my father did the introductions, Second Auntie's face betrayed a gamut of emotions that defy putting into words. None of us would have believed that we would meet for the first time under such circumstances.

The purpose of my trip did not concern Second Auntie. During supper, she was icy and aloof and occupied herself only with refilling the rice bowls and the dishes and keeping in line the eighteen-year-old retarded twins who only seemed capable of making a lot of noise. After supper, I slowly put my cards on the table, so to speak. I said that after the Suzhou factory sent people to raid our home, my mother had suffered a heart attack. A few more raids would be the death of her.

Second Auntie put in, "That's better than what happened to my head."

I continued, "My brother is graduating from college this year. Because of his family background, he may be assigned to Heilongjiang Province in the northeast, but he has severe asthma."

Father said with a sigh, "Asthma runs in the family. Your grandfather suffered from it every winter. I often cough through the night."

Trying to steer the conversation toward my purpose, I went on to say that not only was my brother facing the problem of being given a job assignment, my sister's school had also started to mobilize students to go to the border regions. I added that those with the wrong family background would be the first ones to go.

Picking up on this, Second Auntie said, "I've always said that girls don't need a high school education. If she had taken a factory job, she would have been spared this trouble."

After some hesitation, I decided to break off my sob story. I had planned to tell my father that I had a girlfriend named Xiangzhu, who was from a family of the right background going back three generations, and that her parents were quite frosty to me, afraid that I, with my odious class background, would bring them disgrace. How I wished I could start over as someone else! After a moment's silence, I hardened my heart and let out the purpose of my trip to Suzhou.

"Therefore, for the sake of the future of her children, Mom has decided to divorce Dad."

After a violent shudder, my father lowered his head until it almost reached his knees. Second Auntie's jaw dropped and stayed that way for quite some time. I averted my eyes and looked outside the window, just as a streak of light shot across the pitch-dark sky. A star must have fallen. For one fleeting moment, I felt that I had brought that star to the ground with my words.

I asked my father to write a power of attorney.

I single-handedly went through the divorce formalities. I met with no obstacles in the Civil Affairs Bureau of Jinchang District. One reason sufficed: polygamy. A capable-looking middle-aged female clerk said with emotion when she was affixing a seal to the divorce agreement, "Your mother didn't know what was good for her! Why did she drag her feet until now? If she had divorced earlier, she could have found another husband. Chinese women!"

I replied inwardly, "If the three of us children didn't push her, she would never have come to you! You are right: Chinese women!"

I delivered one of the two copies of the divorce agreement to my father and Second Auntie in the Wen residence. Neither of them stretched out a hand to take it, so I had to leave it on their square dinner table. I was about to turn and go when Second Auntie stopped me.

"In fact," said she, with tears trickling down her cheeks, "it's been so many years. We are all getting old. Why bother?"

I answered, "My mother did this for our sake."

Wiping her tears, Second Auntie said, "I understand. Tell your mother not to worry. I will take good care of him."

Before I left the Wen residence, I turned around for a look at my father. He was sitting motionless, his head sunk on his chest. I saw white hair on his head.

24

My Mother and Second Auntie

Things in this world often turn out to be more complex than we imagine they will. We tend to pin too much hope on the efficiency of legal procedures. My brother went to Heilongjiang nonetheless, and my sister went to Yunnan Province. Xiangzhu, only your parents, simple-minded enough to put all their faith in legal procedures, acknowledged the validity of the divorce paper and consented to our marriage. So I am the only one who benefited from my parents' divorce.

This realization bred in me a sense of shame and remorse towards my parents. By way of making it up to them, I went to Suzhou whenever an opportunity presented itself, to see Father and bring back to Mother some vivid details of his life, playing the messenger between them. In the year following their divorce, on the day of my wedding, I spent the whole morning delivering two catties of wedding candies to Suzhou. I remember that they were the hard Vitamin C candies popular at the time. My father does not like soft candies that stick to the teeth.

It was about seven o'clock in the morning when I arrived in Suzhou. I saw Father the moment I turned onto Quanfu Road. He was sweeping the street with a bamboo broom whose stick was much taller than he was. He was using a great deal of force but doing a poor job of it, savagely sweeping the dust up into the air. One pedestrian did not dodge quickly enough and was hit in the rear with scraps of paper and other sweepings. The man stopped in his tracks, gnashing his teeth. To my surprise, Father also stopped and glowered at the man in a face-off. I didn't dare draw near them because I recognized the man to be

Second Auntie's brother.

Later I heard Father say that their dialogue went like this:

"Enemy of the people! Behave yourself!"

"You son of a bitch! Show your face in my home, if you have the guts!"

Second Auntie's brother had grown up with her. Her kindness to him was known to every resident of Quanfu Road. At Zhenhua Factory, he was in fact the manager, as he himself knew only too well, but later, my father became the exploiter and he the exploited. My father always tried to make the best of the situation and did not take it to heart, but, amazingly enough, Second Auntie's brother took the class struggle seriously. Whenever there was no one around, Second Auntie would curse him to his face in the most unkind and nasty words, but softly, for the benefit of his ears only. Afraid that Mrs. Xuan would retaliate if he went too far, he swallowed the humiliation.

When I described the scene I had witnessed to my mother, she said with a long, drawn-out sigh, "To penalize your father by having him sweep the street is to humble him in the dust on Quanfu Road. This is so hurtful to a proud man like your father!"

Two years later, when my brother returned from the Northeast on home leave, he got off at Suzhou and stayed at the Wen residence for one night. Upon returning to Shanghai, he said to my mother, "There's nothing you need to worry about. That old woman Wen can't be nicer to the old man! When I was there yesterday evening, they were having supper, with four stir-fried courses and one soup, complete with meat and vegetables, and the nicest presentation, aroma, and flavor. Suzhou people are the best epicures. That old woman is quite a good cook. The old man has gotten stronger through physical labor and at each meal, drinks two *liang* of sorghum liquor over a large bowl of rice. He eats more than I do!"

"Does he still have to sweep the streets every morning?" asked my mother.

"This morning the old woman did it for him, because I was there. She got up before daybreak and boiled two kettles of water. Doesn't the old man like a cup of tea in the morning? It was jasmine tea. I heard that it was sent quietly by Big Sister's daughter. Big Sister is at the 'May 7th Cadre School' in Northern Jiangsu. Her husband is with her. Before the morning tea was over, the old woman had finished sweeping the streets and was back at home with a bag of sesame pancakes and deep-fried twisted dough sticks. She herself always eats pickles over rice boiled in hot water, but goes out to buy dim sum for Dad every morning!"

At this point, Mother turned to me and said these puzzling words: "Next time you go to Suzhou, be sure to thank her for me!"

How could I obey such an order? In 1975, I took a group of student workers, peasants, and soldiers to the Suzhou and Kunshan region to study some Ming dynasty ruins. I took some time off and spent one night at the Wen residence. My father was already in his sixties. His capitalist status notwithstanding, the factory transferred him back to the technology department to resume his old job of wool-blending quality control. He didn't have to carry sacks anymore. By this time, his hair had turned all white, his back was bent, and his hearing almost completely gone. As I told him about his Shanghai family at the top of my voice, Second Auntie listened on placidly as she darned a tank top of his by the dim light of the main hall that was falling into decay. She had retired long ago, yielding her post to my retarded little brother, and had, early on, married off his twin sister, who had oversize hands and feet but was less retarded, to a peasant of Huqiu People's Commune. With four or five grandchildren now, she had the kind look of a contented woman. We chatted late into the evening. When I gave a yawn, she immediately left the main hall and brought me a basinful of warm water for me to wash my feet with. I rose in consternation.

"You shouldn't have gone to such trouble!" I said.

"It's no trouble at all. Talking about you Shanghai kids makes your dad happy. Only you and your brother in the Xuan family are successful college graduates, because your mother is educated, unlike me. I'm just a lowly, uneducated person. Go ahead, wash your feet. I'll carry the used water out."

However pleasing these words sounded, I didn't dare relay them to my mother, just as I would never convey my mother's gratitude to Second Auntie. Whatever their differences, they shared one thing in common: Each thought my father belonged to her alone. The legal procedures did not put an end to Mother's sense of ownership over Father. On the other hand, the legal procedures acknowledged Second Auntie's de facto status as wife. Each of them took herself to be my father's one and only legitimate wife. Second Auntie with her narrow mind and intolerance was able to praise her rival and her rival's sons so generously precisely because of her sense of victory and contentment, and her legitimate status as the one and only wife in name as well as in fact.

As Second Auntie reached for the basin, offering to dump the water that I had just washed my feet with, I strenuously resisted her. When both of us were tugging at the wooden basin made by my now deceased grand uncle, I suddenly realized that Second Auntie's exceptional cordiality to me came from that evening ten years earlier—the evening when I produced the petition for divorce that my mother had signed under the coercion of us three children. I had fulfilled the greatest wish of Second Auntie's life—to be the one and only legitimate wife.

25

My Father and Second Auntie

No one could have foreseen the tremendous changes in Chinese politics that occurred in the year 1976, changes that miraculously affected the structure of the Xuan family three years later.

That year, Father got permission to retire. To him, retirement was as good as an amnesty. In fact, he was not eligible for amnesty because his was not a political case. He was neither a Rightist, nor a Trotskyist, nor a member of the Hu Feng counterrevolutionary clique. Whatever the changes in fortune, however many people had their "class enemy" labels removed, he never made the list for an amnesty. In his sixties now, he had long passed the age of "learning the Decree of Heaven" and therefore he pinned his hopes of change on retirement. However, retirement in his case was not to be had easily because over the last ten years or so, he was throughout the factory the only class enemy who had been officially put under surveillance. Wouldn't his retirement mean that class struggle had been extinguished? The factory authorities referred his case to the municipal bureau. The bureau officials couldn't make up their minds, either. It was only when the Central Committee of the Communist Party declared the end of political campaigns that my father's application was finally approved. He was almost seventy when he received the bright red retirement certificate.

To everyone's surprise, within one month of his retirement, he made a premeditated move. Carrying a large traveling bag filled with his clothes and everyday articles, and looking as if he had long-term plans in mind, he returned to Shanghai after a thirteen-year absence, while

Second Auntie was away with her youngest daughter who had just given birth.

My mother had led a quiet life for thirteen years. After raising my son and daughter, she busied herself with my niece and my nephew whom my brother and sister, living outside of Shanghai, had entrusted to her care. Upon my father's return, she was as alarmed as if she were in the presence of "raging floods and wild beasts." She served Father a cup of tea to keep him occupied, and then, in a fluster, she called me by phone and told me to quickly go to her place, sounding as horrified as she would if she were crying, "The Japanese are coming!"

Father was sitting with his head hung low, like a convict awaiting sentencing. When he saw me, he hastened to stand up. He was much shorter than I was. This was the first time I discovered that age shortens people. With one arm around my niece and one arm around my nephew, Mother kept wiping tears from her eyes. The two little ones stared at the stranger as if watching a freak show.

Father had gone completely deaf, but his

mind was still every bit as sharp as before. He was wearing hearing aids that, as I learned later, were a gift from Big Sister. His disconcertion was mixed with his innate stubbornness. His pleading was eloquent. There was no way I could refute him or turn him down.

"I want to live in Shanghai," he said. "I have a pension. I don't need anyone to support me. I'm old. I can't leave your mother again. How many more years do we have? The divorce papers came through during the Cultural Revolution. Aren't people saying that those ten years of turmoil are to be totally and thoroughly repudiated? What's more, even if I'm a divorced man, I can still come to Shanghai to visit my children, as stipulated by the Marriage Law."

"What's to be done about Second Auntie?" I had to interrupt him. I recalled the dim light of the main room in a state of disrepair and Second Auntie's contented expression.

"I've been with her for a good thirteen years!" said my father without a trace of conscience in his voice. "How many more thirteen years do I have?"

"What do my Suzhou brothers and sisters think?"

"Why should I listen to them?" Father raised his voice. "The decision is ours!"

I lapsed into silence. I recalled how I had made decisions for my parents thirteen years earlier. How stupid of me to bring up this subject now!

Turning to Mother, I asked, "Mom, what do you think?"

No sooner were the words out of my mouth than I realized they were superfluous. The divorce was against my mother's wish. Now that Father was over the hill, would she reject him?

My father stayed.

A week later, Big Sister sent me a telegram, saying, "Suzhou Mom gravely ill. Make Dad return immediately."

Mother and I insisted that Father return to Suzhou without delay.

"This can't be true!" said Father as he read the telegram over and over again, with suspicion written on his face. "She likes playing tricks."

"But the telegram came from Number-One. She doesn't play tricks," said Mother.

I resolutely handed my father a train ticket while thinking to myself that Second Auntie, with her toughness, her passion, and her high blood pressure, probably would not be able to survive this blow from her loved one.

I was not mistaken. The very day Second Auntie returned to Quanfu Road from my youngest sister's home in the countryside and learned that my father had fled to Shanghai, she had a brain hemorrhage. She was found lying on the floor by the side of an open trunk, looking as if she was trying to find something. My fourth sister, the primary school teacher, happened to have returned to her mother's home at this moment and, without wasting any time, sent her to the hospital.

For several days in the emergency room of the hospital, she did not move even once, nor did she utter a word. My father rushed to the hospital. As he saw her lying there looking more dead than alive, his heart ached. It was only when he grabbed her hands and called "Xiuzhu" a few times that two large teardrops fell from her eyes.

Then my father's eyes happened to rest upon the diamond ring, glittering on the ring finger of Second Auntie's now stiff left hand— the ring that she had bought with gift money after their fifteen-table wedding banquet.

26

My Big Brother, Big Sister, and I

During the Cultural Revolution, only one member of the Xuan family was not implicated by my father, and that was my big brother.

Every time my thoughts dwell on this, I am overwhelmed by Heaven's fairness. I'm not saying that every person related to my father should come to grief because of him, but if my big brother who was not related by blood to my father was also implicated, just because of the claim "Like begets like," that would have done my big brother too great an injustice. Luckily, after my grandfather's funeral, a widow whose uncle was a production brigade

leader of a neighboring village took a liking
to him and made him a "live-in" husband.
Even though he had left the Xuan Family
Village, he was still among "unfruitful hills
and unfriendly waters." However, just as the
saying goes, "Trees die after moving; people
prosper after relocating." From that time on,
he began to thrive. A local clothing factory
was contracted out to him and his wife. With
its line in coarse acrylic jackets and trousers
meant for the wear and tear of outdoor labor
in cold climates, the factory is not expected to
meet stringent demands for quality. With his
wife in charge of miscellaneous things having
to do with the factory and he himself in charge
of supplies and sales, they make much more
money than we do. Last year, when he came
to Shanghai because Father was critically ill,
he said that they had long been living in a
three-story house. Look at me! I've just been
allotted a three-bedroom apartment, and on
an exceptional basis at that!

My big brother is not a man of vision,
but he got that small factory on the brink of

bankruptcy as early as 1983, which makes him one of the first peasants to run a factory since the beginning of the Reform and Opening-up. He had followed Big Sister's advice. She was the one pulling strings behind the scenes. On her trip escorting my grand uncle's cremated ashes back to Anhui for re-burial, she stayed with my big brother. Upon hearing that there was a financially beleaguered factory in the area, straightaway she made plans and guided my big brother and his wife in taking it over. My sister-in-law was the one who made the final decision. She is a very capable woman with a mind of her own, said to be not any less shrewd than my grandmother. My big brother at the time was not able to make up his mind. This is quite understandable, since he takes after my grandfather.

By the way, the acrylic needed by my big brother's factory was supplied by Mr. Zhou the teacher, who is now a consultant for the Jinshan Petrochemical Works.

In 1983, I also received directions from Big Sister and accomplished another major mission. She had been reinstated, but transferred to another department, to be responsible for the imports and exports of the city of Suzhou. In the summer of that year, she came to Shanghai for a conference and called me by phone, telling me to meet her in her hotel. She had gained weight and looked even more imposing. She had only half an hour for me. Upon learning in our chat about family matters that I had been promoted to lecturer, that my younger brother had been transferred back to Shanghai, and that my younger sister was now a factory director in Yunnan, she broke into a happy smile, looking more like a mother than a sister. Pointing at a large bag, she said, "I've brought this from Suzhou for Mom and Dad. It's filled with food and clothes. There's also a set of hearing aids. The ones Dad is using now are too old-fashioned, and should be replaced. You take the bag to them. I honestly have no time." At this point, she looked me in the eye and asked with an ever so slight smile hovering on her lips, "So you handled their divorce? Acting on their behalf?"

In a flash, there came back to me the memory of my taking matters into my own hands and selling my parents' mahogany bed many years earlier. At the time, she had used the same tone with me and wore the same smile.

My voice faltered. "At that time … It wasn't entirely me … I thought …"

Still smiling, she said, "Hasn't it occurred to you to make another trip to Suzhou? The Civil Affairs Office of Jinchang District remains on Stone Street. It hasn't moved."

"So … you mean, they should apply for restoration of their marriage?"

"Yes."

"Is it necessary? At their age …"

"What a fool you are!" She pointed at me with a finger. Surprisingly, I had the sensation of being pressed on the tip of my nose. She continued, "You still don't understand."

Xiangzhu, I am not that foolish. With Big Sister pointing me in the right direction, I knew what to do. I spent a week's time making preparations. I made inquiries about the right formalities and sought the opinion of my parents. Observing the teenager-like joy and bashfulness in their wrinkled faces, I understood why Big Sister lamented that I didn't understand. I took them to Wang Kai's Portrait Studio on Nanjing Road for one-inch photos, seven duplicates each, to be affixed to the various forms. I took back from them the divorce certificate that I had handed them, one copy each, years earlier. I was startled to see that what Mother produced from her trunk with trembling hands was a thin and long scroll, with one copy of the certificate atop the other. Lying in between was the colored family photo taken before my younger sister was born. I did not dare to ask how the photograph that had been taken by the "rebels" and put on a class struggle exhibition had managed to return miraculously to my mother's trunk. I believe the story behind it would take another whole night to tell. When I felt that everything was ready and victory was certain, I went to Suzhou.

The elderly woman behind the marriage

registration desk in the Civil Affairs Bureau was the very one who had lamented "Chinese women!" I handed her all the required documents. Evidently she didn't remember me. With a business-like air, she examined every item.

"Where are the parties concerned?" she asked.

"My father has gone completely deaf. Even if he came here, he wouldn't have heard you. Plus, he's caught a bad cold. My mother has hypertension and had a minor stroke recently. So she shouldn't leave the house."

"How are you related to them?"

"I'm their son." So saying, I smoothed out the family photo. Pointing at the plump boy leaning clumsily against my mother's knee, I continued, "This is me."

The soft-colored photo had turned a little brownish with erosion over the years, adding a sweet warmth to it. The elderly clerk with speckled hair examined it with interest. With a smile spreading over her otherwise stern face, she asked, "Is that your mother? How many years ago? She was so pretty! Your father was a dashing young man, too!" Turning her eyes to me, she said, "Hey! You look exactly like him!"

Quickly she affixed the government seal on both bright red marriage licenses with gilded characters on their brocade covers.

I almost ran all the way to the post office on Stone Street.

My young nephew answered the phone. "Grandpa and Grandma are out watching a show. Grand uncle gave them the tickets."

That was a reference to Second Auntie's brother-in-law.   After retirement, he often visited my parents and still found a lot in common to talk about with my father.

"Well," I hesitated. "Well, after Grandpa and Grandma come back, tell them …"

"Uncle, hurry up! Long-distance calls are expensive!"

He was one shrewd little Shanghainese!

"Tell them, I've got their marriage license!"

"What?" He was a child, after all.

"Marriage license! Don't you know what a

marriage is?" I raised my voice, feeling both amused and irritated. "A marriage begins with a wedding, where people celebrate with candies and firecrackers."

"Who's having a wedding?"

"That's none of your business! Just tell Grandpa and Grandma that I've got their marriage license!"

Conclusion

I suddenly realized that Xiangzhu had not moved for a long time as she lay by my side, her head pillowed on my arm. After having listened to my story the whole night through without any sleep, she must have been tired. I stopped talking.

"What happened next?" she asked. I could feel her warm breath on my neck. So she had been wide awake!

"Do I need to tell you what happened later?" I gave a yawn. "Haven't you seen how much my parents enjoy each other's companionship year in year out? What I've been telling was history, not the present. The present doesn't need explanations, and can't be explained."

"You do know how to keep secrets, don't

you! I always thought that Auntie Peach and Second Auntie were your father's sisters-in-law, and Big Sister was your cousin!"

"Lying is a talent that comes with birth, and circumstances sometimes give rise to lying. I lied out of a sense of deep shame in my heart."

"Your self-analysis is incisive enough." Xiangzhu gave me a kiss. "Now I know why you made so many index cards on the same subject."

We fell into a prolonged silence. When the first rays of dawn landed on the index cards spread all over my bedside, I drifted off to sleep, but I woke up again when Xiangzhu said under her breath, "So, at long last, your mother has become his number-one wife, his one and only!"

Oh well, this is how women understand things!

Stories by Contemporary Writers from Shanghai